CELEL

MW01244791

Celebrating with *GRACE*

© 2021 EJ Brock
Published by EJ Brock

ISBN: 978-1-949767-14-8

ACKNOWLEDGEMENTS

E George, I could never pull a single book off without your continued support. I don't know what I would do without you.

And to my womb mate, *E Brock*. Girl, you are my ride or die soul mate. You are that special part of me. Thank you for always supporting and pushing me. Thank you for reading and questioning every scenario for continuity.

Z Jones and *Wanda Parks*, I thank you both with undying gratitude.

PROLOGUE

Three years had passed since Floyd was elevated to 'Ultimate Pastor' over a group of *elect* pastors of God, in the United States. Pastor Maulsby had given him the list of the pastors' names, telephone numbers, churches, and their addresses. He was *stunned* speechless over the size of their chosen community. As a son of Maulsby's, he'd already known many of the pastors. He just hadn't known that they were a part of the *Watchers'* select community. Then again, he hadn't realized Pastor Maulsby was either. It was at Carl's murder trial that he found out that Maulsby was a grandson of one of the Ultimate Watchers. And that Tommie was also one of Maulsby's sons in the ministry. Jared became a son that same afternoon. He'd found out about a dozen or so of them when they baptized the Watchers on Michael's island. But those he personally knew was less than one percent of one percent of the number of names on his list.

He'd spent the first half of a dozen years thinking he and his brothers were special. Now he knew that they were, but they weren't the *only ones*.

He couldn't even imagine how that many were hidden from him. Then he heard Holy direct him to read the 19th chapter of 1st Kings. It was the story of Elijah hiding under a tree, in fear of the King of Sidon, Ethbaal's wicked daughter, Jezebel. Of course he knew this story. He'd even preached that the raven bringing Elijah his daily meal was the very first *Grubhub*. Still, he'd long known that the Word of God was living and breathing. And that a passage's meaning, in one's personal life, often breathed new revelations. So, he opened his Bible and read it again. After reading it, he immediately knew what God was reminding him of. It was what He said to Elijah in verse 18, *"Yet I have reserve seven thousand in Israel. All whose knees have not bowed down to Baal, and whose mouths have not kissed him."*

Like Elijah, he'd seriously believed that he and his brothers, and their families, were the *only ones*. That verse had instantaneously put his *arrogant* perspective in check. Some of the ministers on his list even lived with the *Archangels*.

Still, he'd wondered how Maulsby was able to handle this vast number of *elect*, seeing that he had been over both the national *and* international communities. Furthermore, how was *he* going to be able to handle the United States alone. Then Maulsby reminded him, *"You will not be alone, Floyd. Brock will teleport you to and fro. But more importantly, remember what you said when we baptized the Watchers?"* Before he could recall,

Maulsby quoted, *"Yeshua promised that He would be with you all of the way."* That reminder eased his spirit.

With Brock's assistance, he and Mei immediately got about the business of traveling the country, visiting all of the pastors under his leadership. That is all save for *one.* For the last three years, he'd deliberately stayed away from his firstborn, *Grace Tabernacle.*

However, he'd sent a delegation to assist Alden in getting Grace back on course. Every once in a while he had them bring him up to date on how things were going.

EJ Brock
CELEBRATING WITH GRACE

CELEBRATING

WITH

GRACE

EJ Brock
CELEBRATING WITH GRACE

CHAPTER 1

Mark, Candace, Aden, and Betty Jean were sitting at Floyd's kitchen table, eating breakfast. They were there to bring him up to date on Grace Tabernacle's progress. They'd spent the last three years helping the new pastor restructure the church, as well as the leadership.

†††

Floyd wiped his mouth with a napkin and asked, "So how's my firstborn?"

"Matthew is fine," Mark teased.

Floyd hit him with the napkin. "Boy!"

Mark laughed. It had been years in the making, but he loved his newfound relationship with his father. His father respected him for the man that he was, but never let him forget that he was *still* his *baby* boy. He never let him forget that he was one hundred percent in his corner. He'd been concerned about taking on a role at Grace. Mainly because those members knew he'd once been a thorn in the good reverend's side. His father encouraged him by basically quoting a scripture for him to carry with him. *"Let your light shine, son. If you do, they will see your change, and good works. But don't take credit for the change, and don't credit me for it either. They don't need to know all that. Just glorify God and remind them that He's the potter.*" He respected that advice and did just that, whenever those nosey members inquired.

He swallowed the last of his orange juice and then reported, "The membership keeps growing and growing. Pretty much all the old members have come back, and many of them are bringing their neighbors and friends. They love Pastor Gaines, and his preaching style."

Floyd was not surprised. "God sent them a pastor after His heart, son. So of course He would condition their hearts to embrace Alden."

"Many of them say that his preaching reminds them of yours and Jared's style."

"You know the whole *sufficiency* of grace thing," Aden injected.

Mark clapped his hands, laughed, and reported, "Even ole Matlock suit wearing Brotha Benny."

Floyd chuckled. "Y'all need to give Benny a break."

Candace laughed because Mark and Aden always gave each other the side-eye whenever they came face to face with Brother Benny. She changed the subject. "Ms. Lula's new membership class is in the hundreds. Instead of her teaching all of the five-week classes, she only teaches the introductory first week. I teach the second week. Ms. Margaret teaches the third, Ms. Sadie the fourth, and Betty Jean closes it out. That way there is always a first week class and no one has to wait."

That intrigued Floyd because, when he was the pastor, he always taught all of the new members classes. Many times he had people lined up waiting for their turn to start their class. He could actually see why Betty Jean was the *closer*. Back in the day, that woman was just as street as he and Alden had been. He could actually hear her last instruction to her class: *"Don't worry about your past. I ain't always been saved. Back in the day, I drank and partied all night long, all while hanging with the Stones on the side. Believe me when I tell you that when I left the world, it didn't owe me nothing!"*

He looked at her and chuckled. He could honestly say that, every now and again, he missed the days of their common youthful hubris. "That was a brilliant tactic to save the best for last. Was that Lula's or Alden's idea, Betty Jean?"

Betty Jean straight up laughed. The look in Floyd's eyes told her that his mind had just slipped back down memory lane, and her mind immediately followed suit. Back to the days when they, and her husband, thought that they were invincible. Although she was saved now, she still considered those memories *precious*. "Lula suggested it because she knew us back in the day, Floyd. Once she reported what she knew about me to Pastor Gaines, he sanctioned it. They both agreed that my testimony would encourage the once gangbangers to let go of their past."

Floyd's favorite scripture was, *"There is now therefore no condemnation."* He smiled and asserted, "Like the Apostle Paul's, yours, mine, and Alden's pasts are *living* testimonies of the sufficiency of grace."

"Amen, Floyd," she co-signed. Then she waved her hand and acknowledged, "I'm not what I *ought* to be, but I thank God I'm not what I *used* to be."

"You and me *both*, Betty," Floyd professed.

She continued to give her report, "They also agreed that having five teachers would allow people to move quickly towards getting about the business of *their own* ministries."

Floyd furrowed his brows and admitted, "I never once considered my teaching all of the classes was holding them up. I was possibly too arrogant to even consider delegating that task."

"I don't believe that was the case, Uncle Floyd. When you first established the church, you sought out the unchurched. They came to hear what *you* had to say. I believe that people join because of the pastor's message, and they only want to hear from him," Aden rationalized.

"That is true in *some* cases, but not all. Still, it goes to show you that one person does not have to do it all. Like Jesus said, *'The body has many members.'*"

"Pastor Gaines always asks about you. He said that you've never stopped by or visited. He really needs your advice, Dad."

"About?"

Mark, Candace, and Aden roared. Then Mark teased, "You need to call him and let him explain."

He inwardly cringed at the possibility that Benny may be giving Alden a hard time. It bemoaned him that Alden had encouraged Benny to walk down the aisle, and *he* had personally escorted him. He wouldn't have done that under any other circumstance where the pastor stepped down; or was shoved out. He'd done it because he never once considered Benny the *pastor*. Not of Grace Tabernacle, or any other congregation. He shook his head in dismay. "I'll give Gaines a call as soon as we finish our meeting."

Mark saw his mother's shadow moving toward the kitchen. He laughed and very loudly suggested, "You should invite him and First Lady Gaines over for dinner, Dad."

MeiLi rushed in the kitchen when she heard Mark's suggestion. She'd only been in that woman's presence twice, but that was enough to know that she could handle those dogs at Grace. She happily bounced up and down, clapped her hands, and skipped to her husband. "Yes! Yes! Invite them over for dinner, Floyd."

Everybody at the table fell out laughing, including Floyd. His wife got a kick out of Mrs. Gaines's uninhibited tenacity *and* audacity. They'd had a dinner party for all of the ministers, and their wives and husbands, just prior to his going back to gather the members. MeiLi had been awestruck with Mrs. Gaines the minute she opened her mouth. She'd whispered to his mind, *"She'll be able to handle them dogs at Grace, Floyd,"* and chuckled.

Betty clapped her hands and said, "That woman is as unfiltered as I used to be."

"I don't know how you used to be, Betty, but Mrs. Gaines told me that she had no problem calling a shot, where it was played. She unapologetically warned, *'If it comes up in my spirit, it comes out of my mouth,'*" Candace reported and laughed.

"She did not lie. When she put you in your place you knew that you'd been body slammed back to your zip code," Betty said and chuckled.

"I heard her go off on a couple of those old sisters. That woman said, *'Don't try me, sister. Hear me when I tell you, the evil that lives in my flesh is ever present. Trust me, it's just patiently waiting for the opportunity to resurface!'*" Mark reported and howled.

That made Floyd more curious than ever. Now, he couldn't wait to hear what was going on. "That's a good idea. I think I will."

MeiLi laughed right along with Mark. She absolutely loved and admired that woman, because she had more backbone than her and Samantha had combined. She firmly squeezed and shook his shoulders. "Don't think! Just do it, Floyd Walker! And be quick about it. Christmas is in five weeks."

Floyd leaned his head back in her chest and looked up at her. Those loving and trusting eyes of hers got him every single time. "Okay, Mei. I will invite them over for dinner Saturday night."

"Invite Pastor Maulsby and his wife too."

Floyd hit the table and roared. There was as much difference in those two women as there was in a comet and a star. Maulsby's wife spoke gently when getting her point across. Gaines's wife was roaring and blustering. She made the listeners take a step back. "I think you just want to be entertained, Mei."

MeiLi winked at Mark, as she began to knead Floyd's shoulders gently and sensuously. No one was surprised when he closed his eyes and *moaned*. She leaned down close to his ear, and insisted, "Invite them, Floyd!"

Mark cracked up laughing. When they were children his mother could get anything from his father by letting her fingers broker the deal. "Can we come?"

Aden really wanted to be in Pastor Maulsby's presence. In the past, whenever he was around the man he felt the glory of God exuding from him. He decided to sweeten the pie. "If you let us come, I'll get my wife to cook the entire dinner. Including dessert."

Floyd licked his lips. There wasn't a person on the estate who didn't crave Aden's wife, Dee's southern style cooking. Over the years that woman had carved out a catering business, by cooking for one family or another. "That's blackmail, boy!"

Aden nodded, laughed, and said, "Yep!'

Floyd chuckled and agreed, "You have a deal, Aden!"

Then he stood up, wrapped his arms around MeiLi, and kissed her. Her fingers massaging his shoulders had driven him to a state his guests did not need to witness. While gazing in her eyes, he announced, "This meeting is *over.* Don't let the door hit cha."

Mark roared. He loved that his parents still had a vibrant love life. He stood up and sang, "Let's get it on!"

"Mine your business, Mark," MeiLi said without taking her eyes off Floyd.

They all laughed as they exited the back door.

†††

CHAPTER 2

Pastor Alden Gaines was in one of the conference rooms, at Grace, talking with Brother Benny. The founder of Grace, Floyd Walker, had named this particular room *Galilee*, because he said it was the meeting place for restoration *or* separation. He'd taken that idea from Jesus sending word for His disciples to meet Him in Galilee, just prior to His ascension. He liked the concept because it was in Galilee that Jesus's disciples' first saw that He was *still* alive. It restored their faith and the zeal to boldly carry the message of is birth, life, death, and resurrection, throughout the world.

Although he'd had many meetings in this conference room, none were to sever ties. More often than not, members met with him to pour out their souls for their sinful behavior the prior week. He knew that the word said to confess your sins to one another, but good grief! They seemed to be of the mindset that he, as their pastor, could absolve them. Little did they understand, he couldn't even absolve himself.

He was meeting with Benny today, but not for

that *foolery*. Benny had come a *long* ways in his understanding of Christianity, and his behavior bore him out. He came to Bible study, prayer meeting, Sunday school, and Sunday morning service, every week. He couldn't sing a lick, but he came to choir rehearsal. Not to sing, but to bus those who didn't have transportation. He even taught a class at the church every Saturday. Not on the *Bible* per se, but on personal finances, and how they lined up with scripture. Seeing that he was a money man, he mentored them on tithing and offering *first*. He said, *"Pay God ten pennies out of every dollar you are paid. Then pay yourself the next ten pennies. Don't spend it on the newest gym shoes, rims, or computer game, but by saving them for your future. That leaves you eighty pennies to live on. Minus your love offering to our pastor."* Amazingly the class was mostly filled with young men and women. All of them eager to learn how to better themselves, their way of living, and their futures.

During one testimonial service, Benny started his testimony by quoting Paul, *"I count not myself to have apprehended; but this one thing I do, forgetting those things which are behind, and reaching forth unto those things which are before, I press toward the mark for the prize of the high calling of God in Jesus Christ."* Then he wiped his eyes and said, *"Forget my past is what the good reverend whispered in my ear, when he escorted me down the aisle. I've learned that even though time does not stop, through Christ it restarts in each of*

---

our lives." That last statement compelled the musician to softly play "I press on." And in the middle of Benny's testimony, the choir joyously sang out, "For the prize. Eternal life!" He couldn't finish his testimony because the congregation broke out shouting in the aisles. Especially the ex-gangbangers Bill and Dedrick.

Even though he was the new pastor, he couldn't take credit for the renewing of Benny's mind. That was all *Floyd Walker's* doing.

Floyd had walked through the Bible in his last sermon at Grace, three years ago. That sermon pricked the hearts of the leadership and the congregation, alike. Not to mention the ministers seated behind him, including *himself.* More importantly, that sermon had convicted the previous pastor, Brother Benny! That preacher read Benny, and the prior leadership, from in the beginning to Amen. And although Floyd had been downright petty, he chased every word that preceded out of his mouth with *scripture.*

✝✝✝

He was in a meeting with Brother Benny today, because the man just liked talking with him. Every time they had a private one-on-one, he complained that he'd spent his entire life *misunderstanding* God's word. And today was no different...

✝✝✝

"Those old fire and brimstone pastors I grew

up under didn't understand God's word either, Pastor."

"No, they didn't. In fact, they were partly responsible for my joining the Bloods, back in the day."

"Seriously?"

"I was actually born in Indiana, just five miles from this church."

"I didn't know that."

Alden nodded. "My parents moved to California when I was three. As a child, I always went to church because my father lived and breathed the scripture, 'as for me and *my* house'."

"Tell me about it," Benny commiserated and laughed.

"Then my father passed. My mother had never worked, and she really struggled to pay the bills. She went to the church for help several times. They told her that she was an able body and that she should get a job. Then they prayed for her," he reported, and then grimaced at the memory of his mother's tears. "They didn't offer her a slice of bread or a cup of rice. Just a prayer! Prayers don't exactly fill the belly, do they, Benny?"

"Nah, I can't say that it does."

"One day the leader of the gang, in my neighborhood, spotted me in an alley, going through a store's garbage. He asked me why I would do that. I told him I was hungry and stores always throw good food away. Especially day-old bread and canned food that's about to expire," he said and paused. Then he looked at Benny and asked, "You know what he did?"

"What?"

"He sent some of his gangbangers to our house with *bags* upon *bags* of groceries. There was a note inside that promised that they would send us food every week."

"You jiving!"

Alden shook his head. "No, I'm not. And they did just that. Not only that, but the leader took my mother down and got her rushed to the front of the line for welfare and food stamps."

"Did you and your mother continue to go to that church?"

"Not that one, or any other church. That experience taught us that the world was much more compassionate towards the downtrodden than the church. The minute I turned sixteen, I joined that gang."

That story saddened Benny. It reminded him that he'd pushed the church members out too. Not by denying them food, because at his worst, he'd never done that. Nevertheless, pushed out is pushed out. "How do you think that pastor fared in the judgment?"

"The final judgment has not come yet, Benny. However, it is not for me to speculate. When that great day of judgment does come, Yeshua will judge them according to their hearts."

"But the scripture says, 'When I was hungry you didn't feed me.' That still stands today," Benny

---

reminded him.

"That is true. However, you never know if they changed their way of dealing with the poor. As long as there is life there's hope, and a possibility for change." Then he smiled and testified, "Look at how the Lord has changed me. I've gone from gangbanging and disdain for the church to pastoring this one. More to the point, look at *you*, Brother Benny."

"Ain't that the gospel," Benny replied and genuinely smiled. Once he changed, God restored everything he'd lost, and then some. Still, he frowned. "I have a problem I want to discuss with you."

"What's wrong?"

"You know my wife and I remarried."

"Yes." He'd counseled them for two months, but not remarried them. "You guys really should've allowed me to perform the ceremony."

"She wanted to go to the courthouse this time around. She says that she loves the change in me. Nevertheless she is not going back to Butts."

"Butts?"

Benny blushed. "Butts is my last name."

Alden's eyes bucked. Then he reared his head all the way back, stomped his foot, and robustly laughed. "Your last name is Butts, man? Benny Butts!" he squeaked out.

"*Benjamin* Butts. I was named after my enslaved great grandfather. Google him, Alden. His story is amazing."

Alden looked at Benny, hit the desk and squeaked out, "I'll bet you got your *butt* kicked every day, when you were a kid."

Benny nodded. Even now he believed that children can be the cruelest little monsters. He chuckled. "You already know, man. Why do you think I go by Brotha Benny?"

Alden squealed louder. He wondered if Floyd knew that Butts was this cat's name. It certainly fit his past behavior. He wiped his tear-streaked face and chuckled. "I would've kept that a secret too."

"So you agree that it's okay for Jeanetta to continue to go by Jeanetta Wade?"

Alden hunched his shoulders. "What's in a name? You all call my wife Sister Gaines, but that is not her *legal* name."

"What?"

"Antoinette and I have been married over thirty years, and she has *never* carried my last name, man. Her name is Antoinette *Gates,* not *Gaines*."

"That doesn't bother you?"

"No matter what her last name is, she knows that I am the *head* of our house."

Benny went to respond but the phone rang. Alden held up his finger and answered, "Pastor Gaines." Then he furrowed his brows and said, "Floyd!" He listened as Floyd talked and then he said, "See you then," and hung up.

Benny felt the *strife* in Alden's spirit. He didn't ask any questions though. He stood up and said, "I need to run. Ms. *Wade* is probably wondering where I am."

Alden stood up and stretched. He could honestly say that he enjoyed this meeting. And God knows he really liked the *new* Benny. "I have to go too. I'll walk out with you, Butts."

"Please don't call me that in public."

"Does Floyd know your last name?"

"NOPE! Jeanetta and I paid our tithes in *cash*."

Alden roared. The two of them joked and laughed at Benny's name's expense, all the way to their cars. "The next time we have a meeting, I will tell you how the boys in the gangs, in my neighborhood treated me. All because of my *surname*," Benny promised and laughed.

Alden didn't laugh at *that* statement. He knew that childhood experiences shape the man. What that church did to his mother had certainly shaped him. But when God was ready, He reeled him in. Just as He'd done Jonah and the Apostle Paul. And just as He'd done Floyd, and *every other* Pastor, in their elect ministry.

He wondered if Benny's treatment by those gangs was the reason that he'd given Floyd such a hard time. "I look forward to discussing it with you, Benny."

They shook hands and parted ways.

CHAPTER 3

Dee had been cooking in MeiLi's kitchen all morning long. She'd spent fifty percent of the time shooing MeiLi away. "Too many cooks will ruin a meal, Aunt MeiLi."

"I'm just trying to help."

Dee rolled her eyes and grunted. She experienced this every time she cooked at one of the Walker women's houses. One of these days she was going to just flat out refuse to cook for them. She didn't care who the dinner was for. "I appreciate that, but I don't *need* your help."

"You are letting Candace and Betty Jean help."

"I don't have time for this, MeiLi. I've got to finish so that I can go home, shower, and dress. Just let me do what I do. Please!"

Candace laughed at her mother-in-law's defiant expression, and Dee's adamant one. Dee was right, the woman had attempted on several occasions to sneak some of her seasonings in the food. When she wasn't doing that, she was trying to taste everything. She'd told Dee that they should cook the food at her house, and have Mark and Aden bring it. Dee refused, because she didn't want to have to tote her cookware back home afterward. She said that the food needed to be cooked in Muqin's pots, skillets, and pans. Muqin had agreed with Dee, now she was in the way. "I'm just washing the dishes as soon as Dee gets finished with them, Muqin."

"And I'm drying them, and putting them away, so your kitchen won't be cluttered with dirty dishes when our guests arrive," Betty Jean defended.

Floyd walked in the kitchen from the backyard. He immediately sniffed the aroma and smiled. "Everything smells good in here, Dee. It reminds me of Madea cooking Sunday dinner, every Saturday. We couldn't wait to dig in after church."

"Thank you. Now would you *please* get your wife out of here before she ruins it."

Floyd looked at MeiLi and questioned, "What are you doing, Mei?"

"I'm just *trying* to help."

To make amends for his absence, Floyd had decided that the dinner would be in Gaines and his wife's honor. Nothing fancy, just good old fashion southern style food, and hospitality. He instructed Gaines to extend the invitation to his assistant pastor, and his wife. He invited the ministers that lived on the estate, and their wives and husbands, to join them. He'd also invited Maulsby but he

---

declined, citing his calendar was booked through the end of the year. He accepted that excuse, but he suspected that Maulsby was doing to him what he'd done to Gaines. At almost the last minute, he extended the invitation to Brock and Jodi. He reasoned that it was time for Gaines to fellowship with the man who was over the entire community. Plus, it wouldn't hurt to boast that *he* not only lived on Brock's estate but, shared family members with him.

He really wanted this gathering to go off, without a hitch. That meant the meal had to be perfect. It could only be if Dee was allowed to do her thing. He could tell by her expression and tone that MeiLi was working her nerves. "Come out of here, Mei. Dee doesn't *want* your help. And I'm positive she doesn't *need* your supervision."

"I don't require *either* one!" Dee snapped. Then she checked her own attitude. She and MeiLi had come a long way, and she didn't want to ruin their relationship. "I'm sorry, Aunt MeiLi. Will you just set the dining room table?"

MeiLi didn't want there to be bickering between her and Dee either. It wouldn't look right if they were at odds when their guests arrived. Not to mention if word got out, her daughter Symphony would march her butt through the front door and tell her off. She smiled. "Okay. Do you want to use *my* Ming Dynasty china, or Floyd's mother's?"

Candace had noticed her mother-in-law's china in the china cabinet, years ago. It was a dark

---

garnet red with gold dragons slithering throughout. *And* it was absolutely *too gaudy* for her taste. Mark told her that his father bought it for his mother, right after *Spoiler* was born. He said they were only allowed to eat off them on very *special* occasions, like Easter and Christmas. That made no sense to him, her either. In both of their minds every day on this side of the grave was a special occasion. She'd also seen her father-in-law's mother's china in that same cabinet. It was plain white, edged in gold pearls. *And* it was simple, *elegant,* and *stunning.*

Her generation did not see the purpose of china. Nevertheless, Muqin did, and this was her party. She spoke up before Dee could, "Since this is a southern style dinner, I think Dad's mother's plain white china would go better, Muqin."

Dee knew Candace didn't like MeiLi's china, *at all.* Candace had even told Mark that she was *never* going to eat off something that *creepy.* She inwardly chuckled because she knew what no one else did. It was her Grand Mama Girl's old china. Her grandpa Gus had bought it for her one year for Christmas, from a store that was going out of business. Her Grand Mama Girl took one look at it and closed the box back up. She even tried to regift it to Everett's mother a few years later for Christmas. Cora rejected it too. She claimed that since it was a gift from Gus, she couldn't accept it. Plus, she had inherited her own mother's china. Floyd had eventually bought it at one of her grandmother's garage sales. She would never say anything because she didn't know if MeiLi knew where he got it from. Besides, they had never been used, and a gift is a gift. "That's a good point, Candace. We don't want the china to be the conversation piece tonight."

"Bring it in here, MeiLi. I'll wash them," Betty Jean offered.

MeiLi was extremely happy to be doing something. "Coming right up," she replied. Then she rushed in the dining room and started pulling the china out.

Floyd followed MeiLi, but whispered to Dee's mind, *"Carry on. I'll keep my wife busy in the dining room."*

Dee chuckled outloud. *"Thank you so much, Uncle Floyd. I just want everything to be perfect."*

"I have no doubt it will be."

CHAPTER 4

Floyd's and MeiLi's house was lively with their invited guests. They were laughing and chatting, while enjoying a glass of wine from Brock's cellar. The Temptations singing in the background, on Spotify, was a reminder that this was the holiday season. Unfortunately, everybody was there *except* the guests of honor.

"Do you think they have gotten lost, Floyd?" MeiLi asked.

Charity was wondering the same thing. They were supposed to be there at four o'clock, for cocktail hour. It was already fifteen minutes after. "This place *is* off the beaten path," she reminded them.

"This time of day they could be stuck in traffic on I-65," Sal suggested.

Samantha looked at Jared and chuckled. Her husband was as old school as it got. He didn't want an electronic Bible, Ebook, *or* map. He said that he liked the feel of paper in his hands. Then he teased that she should be happy that he embraced the cell phones. God knows she was. "Hopefully he's not the type of man that is too old fashion to use a GPS."

"It's a manly man's thing," Jared retorted and chuckled.

"There ain't nothing like an old fashion paper atlas. Is it?" Tommie asked. Then he and Jared bumped fists.

Gloria looked side eyed at Samantha and smacked her lips. "Tommie would rather use a paper map even at night, with a flashlight, than turn on our GPS."

"What? That's just *stupid*. Why would you prefer that when your car has a GPS?" Mark asked.

"That will bring you right up to the door at that," Aden injected.

"And what happens when, and *if*, the satellite fails?" Floyd asked. "You young folks don't even know how to use a map, do you?"

"You know good and well they don't," Brown answered. "If the satellite did go down, they wouldn't be able to find their way off this subdivision," he mocked.

"As long as Uncle Brock don't need GPS to teleport us, we won't have to either," Mark came right back.

Brock had just taken a sip of wine, and momentarily choked at Mark's comeback. He spoke to everybody with his mind, *"You got that right, nephew."* When he finally stopped coughing, he slapped both Mark and Aden a high five. They all cracked up laughing, and then started bantering back and forth. Brock, the women, Mark, and Aden, against the old schools.

Brock liked *punctuality,* even if it was just a party. He was getting a little concerned because it was snowing hard in the city. Not having a link with Gaines, he decided to go through Floyd's memories to see where the man was. If they were in fact just lost, or stuck in traffic, he'd direct Gaines's mind on which way to go. He knew that Gaines wouldn't be afraid because that preacher had been a part of their community for years. When he spotted them, he smiled and announced, "Chill out! They've just turned off the interstate onto the preserves." Then he opened the gates with *his* mind.

Gaines shook Floyd's hand the moment he walked through the door. Then he looked around and said, "You're squatting on some prime real estate, Floyd. That forestry we just drove through is *amazing.* I've never seen anything like it. Not only is it snowing everywhere but here, the trees are still green. As soon as I grow up, man."

Floyd laughed. Then he said, "I believe you already know everybody. Those preserves and most of the real estate belongs to *Brock.* You met him at our meeting with Maulsby three years ago."

Gaines extended his hand to Brock, "Yes. I remember. It's good to see you again."

"Same here. This is my wife, Jodi."

Gaines shook her hand and greeted her. He

was still holding her hand when Floyd said, "Brock is the first Nephilim ever born. He is the Ultimate of Ultimate Watchers, *Seraphiel*."

Gaines squeezed down hard on Jodi's hand, and at the same time questioned Brock, "You're Samjaza's offspring?"

Brock nodded. "The first of thirty-one."

Gaines bore down even harder on Jodi's hand. "Thirty-one!"

Jodi yelped, "Ouch!" and tried to pull her hand away.

Gaines jumped when he heard Brock growl. He immediately released Jodi's hand. "I am so sorry. I'm just in a little shock."

"That's alright," Jodi assured him. Then she took the liberty of introducing herself to his wife, and the other couple. "I'm Jodi Brock. This is my husband, Brock.

"Good to meet you. I'm Alden's wife, Antoinette Gates."

"Hello, I'm Capricious Sinclair. This is my husband, Sterling Sinclair."

Floyd had been messing with Gaines and had not even noticed who else had come in his house. He whipped around and said, "Capri? *You're* the Assistant Pastor?"

She laughed. "Yes, Floyd. It's good to see you again."

Floyd scowled at Mark, Candace, Aden, and Betty Jean. He'd never asked them who the assistant pastor was. Still, they should have volunteered the information. "Did all of you conveniently forget to share that with me?"

They laughed and pointed at Alden. "He told us not to, Dad."

Floyd squinted at Alden. "What? Why?"

Alden grunted. "I have not heard a peep out of you since you announced I was the new pastor. Your trifling butt even changed your cell number."

Floyd went to explain, but Gaines kept griping, "Three years later and *I* still have not been *installed*. I can't install Capri because I am not *official*. What in the devil's homestead is wrong with you, Walker?"

Floyd stared at Mark and squinted. Mark spoke up to defend himself, Candace, Aden, and Betty Jean, "We didn't know *that* was what he wanted to talk to you about, Dad."

Betty didn't like the way this was going. They'd been with Alden for three years. Neither he nor Antoinette mentioned anything about an installation service, or their *need* for one. Capri hadn't mentioned it either. "There is no way we would've kept *that* to ourselves, Floyd."

Formalities never crossed Floyd's mind. He wasn't installed at Grace, or at Redeeming Love, because he was the founder of both. It hadn't occurred to him to install Jared because God assigned him. God had assigned Alden too, but Alden served *humans,* with human customs, rituals, *and* doctrines.

Out of nowhere, Holy inundated his mind's

eyes with scenes of Moses *consecrating* Aaron as High Priest at the door of the temple, in front of the Israelites. He closed his eyes in remorse because consecrating and installing was the *same* thing. "Come on. Y'all sit down and let me try and explain myself."

†††

Once everyone was seated, Floyd started filling, and refilling, their wine glasses. Brock felt his dismay and eased his spirit. Then he took the wine bottle from him, and insisted, "Have a seat, Floyd, I got this." Floyd smiled and took his seat. When Brock finished, he refilled his own glass, and took his seat next to Jodi.

Floyd tilted his glass towards Alden. "I wasn't ignoring you, Alden."

"What would you call it then, Floyd? We know that you have crisscrossed the country, visiting the churches in our district," Antionette pointed out.

Floyd glanced at her with a lopsided smile. Then he chuckled in Brock's mind, and said, *"It appears that the ministers under my leadership have a grapevine that mirrors the one on the estate."*

Brock roared. *"Indeed."*

MeiLi enjoyed Antoinette's brazenness, but not when it was directed at Floyd. She'd put her own sons out of her house for disrespecting her husband. She had no problem doing the same thing to Antoinette. "You or Alden could've had Mark dial Floyd's number from his cell phone, at any time, *Ms.* Antoinette."

Antoinette's head literally snapped back in surprise, at the *tone* of MeiLi's voice. She immediately regrouped and snarked, "We *could* have, but we assumed that Floyd *did not* want to hear from us."

"You're old enough to know what happens when you *assume,*" MeiLi came right back at her.

Floyd raised his hand to stop them. He knew, like everyone in this room did, that MeiLi would go to the mat for him. All the wives on the estate would for their husbands. "You're right, Antoinette. With Brock's help, MeiLi and I have travelled coast to coast. It was for the purpose of introducing ourselves to the pastors that I did *not know,* and, who did not know me. However, I sent a delegate of four to help Alden get Grace up and running. Even though Tommie really could've used them at the boy's club, they've been at Grace for three years. Have they not?"

Alden squeezed his wife's knee. It was their silent communication for her to hush. Then he answered Floyd, "Yes, and they have been a great help."

Floyd slowly nodded and crossed his legs. "I've witnessed too many times where the pastor stepped down, because of age, yet remained at the church. Conflict arises each and every time. In some cases it's because the members go behind the new pastor's back to gripe to the old pastor. A lot of times it is the old pastor's refusal to completely relinquish the reins. He continuously asserts his *non-existent* authority over the new pastor. More often than not in front of the entire congregation. Ofttimes the new pastor just gives up and resigns. His departure more often than not causes a split. The members who were on the new pastor's side, follow him. The ones who started the mess eventually seek out other houses of worship. That's because the old pastor insists that he is *still retired*, so to speak. I often wanted to call those pastors and say, *'Don't do it, man! Send those heathens on down the road.'* To this day, I *still* feel sorry for those pastors who accepted those troublemakers' membership."

Gaines squealed, "I hear ya, Floyd!"

Floyd grunted. "Unfortunately, it's the seniors who are the most wounded. They just go home and *stay*. That's what happened to Grace, after God called Jared out from amongst them. They selected a man who had no more been called than Lucifer. The church fell apart, and eventually dissolved. And they were lost in the wilderness, until God sent *me* to gather *His* flock. Once they came back, I introduced them to the shepard that God had sent to them. *You*, Alden."

He paused long enough to take a sip of his wine. Then he continued, "Once I did what God told me to do, I walked away and never looked back. I immediately changed my cell phone number. Not because I held animosity or no longer cared about Grace, or you. It was because I *did* care, and still *do*, man. They came to Christ under *my* leadership, Alden. They came because they knew my *gangbanger* past. They believed that if God could reach down deep and choose *this* marred clay, there might be *hope* for *them*."

"Go on and preach anyhow, Floyd," Sal shouted before Aden could.

"I didn't, and don't, want my beloved *firstborn*, Grace, to ever split or be lost again. I certainly didn't want you to experience what I knew was bound to happen. I didn't want them calling me complaining when things didn't go their way. You don't need my input muddying the water, any more than Jared does. Although Grace is, and will forever be, *my* bitter cup, *you* are the shepard that *God* sent to shepherd them."

Alden took a sip of his wine and sighed. Everything Floyd had just said was spot on. He experienced that at his *previous* church. On the day he was set to announce his resignation, God sent Maulsby to inform him that He was sending him to Grace. "I know that in the beginning the members were sad that you were not coming back, Floyd. I saw it in their eyes. They love you, and hoped you were staying."

"I saw it in all of their faces, too, Alden. Even as they made their way to the altar," Jared co-signed.

"We all saw and felt it. That's why it was imperative for me to stop all communication with them, *and* you," Floyd explained.

"In the end, they decided to stay. To give not

just me but each other a chance. I won't lie. It was a struggle at first, but it has been three years and they've more than adjusted. I can honestly report that I have not lost one member. Margaret is still the secretary, Lula is still our new members lead teacher. Frank Leavy is my *head* deacon and accountability partner. His son, Steve is still over the parking ministry. Our pews are filled *every* Sunday. Even some of your old gang members have joined."

"So I've heard."

"You really should make an appearance. If for no other reason than to finally install Alden," Antoinette suggested in a softer tone.

"I will most definitely do *that*, as soon as earthly possible," Floyd promised.

Alden nodded and then he looked at Jared. He knew from his last visit that Jared had taken over the church on these grounds. "Just out of curiosity, have you installed Jared? And how have you dealt with the members of his congregation?"

"No. I have not installed Jared, or Sal. Truthfully, it never crossed my mind to do it. So you see, you are in good company," Floyd said and chuckled. "The majority of the people that live in this community are either my family members, or the Indiana *Watchers*." Then he pointed at Charity and said, "She is my brother, Smith's *oldest* daughter. Her husband, Sal, is the Ultimate Watcher, Adabiel's grandson." Then he pointed at Jodi. "She is my oldest brother, Hezekiah's *youngest* daughter. My daughter, and most of my nieces, are married to

Watchers, Alden."

Alden looked at Brock and Jodi and said, "Get out!"

Brock chuckled. "My team and I needed a large house of worship. So we had one built on the estate grounds."

Alden smirked. "I've been in the church. I'm talking about you and other Watchers being related to Floyd, and his brothers."

Brock laughed again. Then he wrapped his arm around Jodi's shoulders. "Actually the Walker brothers are the descendants of the Ultimate Watcher, over Chicago, Satariel."

"Don't forget that Mama is Satariel's, Kobabiel's, *and* Spirit Warrior's descendant," Jodi reminded Brock.

"True that."

"Not just Watchers, Alden. My friend, Anita Foster, in Galveston, Texas, is married to the Archangel Jeremiel. She told me that her father and Jodi's father are first cousins," Capri injected.

Jodi smiled and confirmed, "They are."

"Pri told me that you know Jophiel and Raguel, Brock. Do you guys spend any time with them, and their mates?" Sterling asked.

Brock smiled. "Of course I know them. They are my uncles. We haven't seen them in a while. How are Brandi and Wanda doing?"

"They're good. They, and their mates, plan to be in attendance at Pri's installation."

Alden was wondering why he had been kept

in the dark regarding these connections. "The only Archangel I've ever met is Michael."

"Michael is here all the time. He is Brock's *adopted* father. That makes him my father-in-law, and our children's grandpa," Jodi bragged.

Antoinette stared at Jodi and questioned, "The General in God's army?"

Jodi and Brock nodded. "One and the same."

"He was at your introduction service, Alden. There were six Archangels watching over the children, in the children's church," Capri informed him.

"Say *what?*"

She nodded and then went on to tell everybody how long she, and Sterling, had known them. And how they rescued her and Jodi's cousin, Anita Foster. That kicked off a vigorous conversation.

Dee finally stood up and said, "I spent all morning in the kitchen preparing a southern style meal for our guests. It's six o'clock. Can we move the conversation to the dining room?"

Everyone said, "Yes," and stood up.

CHAPTER 5

Dee and Floyd had agreed that the dinner would be self-serving buffet. Mainly because she'd slaved all day and didn't want to serve *anybody*, but Aden. They lined rows of covered chafers on the breakfront, with tea light candles to keep the food warm, along with serving tongs. MeiLi placed the china plates and saucers at the front of the line. Candace and Betty Jean took care of putting the wine and water glasses, coffee cups, flatware, napkins, and *Chinese* placemats on the table. Seeing that the tablecloth was white linen and the china was white and gold, the red mats actually looked good. They offset it with solid gold candleholders and red candles as the center piece.

As soon as Mark rolled back the Chinese screens to the dining room, the savory aroma accosted Alden's nostrils. He went to cross the threshold, but MeiLi blocked the entrance. Then she looked at Floyd and squinted. Floyd and Jared both roared and apologized, "Sorry, MeiLi."

Then Floyd pointed down the hall and

explained, "MeiLi won't allow anyone in her kitchen or dining room until they wash their hands."

Alden looked to see that everybody was standing in line to, or coming out of, what he assumed was the bathroom. That is except him, Antoinette, Floyd, and Jared. He sheepishly defended, "It isn't that we don't wash our hands before eating. We just usually wash them in the kitchen sink, or the wet bar in our dining room."

"It was our way of being sure that our children washed their hands. Over time it just became the norm," Antoinette explained. "But when in *Rome!*"

They wordlessly got in line.

When everybody was seated, Mark said grace. As soon as he finished, Alden looked across the table at Dee and questioned, "Did I understand you to say that you cooked this meal?"

"Yes, sir."

He looked back down at his plate at the smothered oxtails in a red wine gravy over rice, *fried* pork ribs, a mixture of turnup and mustard greens, candied yams, and mac and cheese. Hot water cornbread, and buttery yeast rolls, were piled on a saucer. He took the liberty of sampling everything. Then his eyes rolled back in his head and he mumbled, "I haven't had fried pork ribs since my mother died, over thirty years ago."

"None of us had ever even *heard* of them,

until Dee introduced us to them," Jared informed him.

"My wife goes from house-to-house, once a month, cooking them for everybody on the estate," Aden bragged.

Alden was truly feeling a sense of nostalgia because the ribs tasted just like his *mother's*. Even the *batter*. "You don't use all-purpose flour, do you?"

Dee shook her head. "I fry everything in cake flour, because it's lighter and flakier."

"I know darn well you do. My mother used cake flour for that very reason. Plus, it doesn't hold as much oil."

"These oxtails with this onion and mushroom gravy ain't short stepping either," Sterling injected.

Alden always completely ate each dish before starting another. It was so that he could appreciate each one in their own right. He was also old school and didn't use utensils unless necessary. He'd saved the greens until last because...

"I'm about to get real country up in here, y'all," he unabashedly forewarned. Then he crumbled his cornbread in his greens and ate them with his hand. When he finished, he sucked the juice off of his fingers, looked back at Dee, and asked, "Who in the *world* taught you how to cook, young lady?"

Dee had watched Alden eat his greens, and she had a big smile on her face. "My Grand Mama Girl was Black. She taught me how to cook soul food. She used to crumble her cornbread in her greens, and then eat them with her fingers too. She said she left no juice behind."

"Her grandmother was Smooth's mother," Floyd injected.

Alden had known *of* Smooth as long as he'd known of Floyd. He glanced at Floyd and back at Dee. "Smooth is your father?"

Dee shook her head and looked to her right. Then she smiled and embraced Salvador's hand. "Sal and Charity are my *parents.* Grand Mama Girl was my grandfather's life mate."

Sal's eyes were glowing with pride when he leaned over and kissed her cheek. "We most certainly are."

Antoinette had enjoyed the meal as much as her husband. "Whenever we are invited to dinner, I always cook a small meal at home because you *never* know," she admitted. "I'm here to tell you that in all of my life, I've never met a woman who could out beat me cooking. Let alone a *White* one! Who, by the way, at first glance looks more like a beauty queen, than a chef! But I must respectfully crown you the *queen of Chefs,* young lady."

Everybody burst out laughing at the way she complimented Dee. Dee blushed. "Thank you."

"Many of our members have no family. Or their families live in other cities or states. We serve lunch every day at the church, so that they can have daily companionship. We also cook Thanksgiving and Christmas dinner at the church, so that they are not alone on the holidays. We pass out flyers inviting the homeless to join us, and they show up in droves. Would you be interested in cooking this year's Christmas dinner?" Antoinette asked.

Alden liked that idea and sweetened the pot, "Name your price."

Living on the estate, Dee knew that this was their season for giving back to the less fortunate. They'd already had several meetings about serving the poor and homeless. "I would be honored, but no price. That is other than your supplying the food."

Alden shook his head. "I insist we pay you, Dee. The Bible says that a servant is worthy of his or her hire."

Sal came to his daughter's defense by quoting Smooth's spiel, "It also says, 'Give and it shall be given unto you by a good measure-'"

Everybody that lived on the estate cut him off by quoting, "Pressed down! Shaken together! It'll run over in your lap!"

"All of the women that live on the estate will assist my daughter," Charity injected.

MeiLi, Betty Jean and Candace were all nodding. "Do you have an approximate head count?" Samantha asked.

"I'll tell you as soon as Dee gives me a price per plate."

"Not one penny," Dee quoted.

"You're not going to win this discussion, Alden. Not with this many women against you," Gloria asserted. "We've been too blessed not to pay it forward."

"These people find great joy in giving back. Don't deprive them of that," Jared stated. "It was their zeal for giving that led to me finding my grandsons and their mother living on the street, a few years ago. I wasn't even aware that I had any grandchildren, man. My son had no idea his wife was pregnant, let alone with *twins*, when they separated."

"What?"

"No clue," Jared added and shook his head. "Let these women do what they do, man."

Alden couldn't *imagine* his children, or grandchildren, sleeping on the cold ground. He nodded and relented. "Two or three hundred people."

"How about this," Brock said and got everybody's attention. "We men will provide the food."

"That's what's up, Unc," Aden said and slapped Mark a high five.

Mark laughed at the looks on their guests' faces. Then he explained, "We do this every year. Normally the women cook and we men deliver it in the city. This way, the food will already be in the city."

Tommie excitedly wiggled his pointer finger and added, "*And* they can sit down at a welcoming table and eat, instead of eating in a cold alley."

"How many do you guys normally feed, Dee?" Capri asked.

"We prepare at least three hundred hot meals for the homeless. Sometimes more. In addition, we also prepare baskets for those who have homes, but struggle to make ends meet."

"Then I would suggest we increase our count to six hundred."

"That's doable."

"So we will be celebrating Christmas at Grace Tabernacle this year," Jodi stated and smiled. Prior to meeting Brock, she'd always enjoyed going to Grace. Especially during the holidays. "I am looking forward to that."

†††

Satisfied, Dee smiled, stood up, and asked, "Who's ready for coffee and dessert?"

Everyone raised their hands. Alden could not wait. He actually clapped his hands when Dee and Candace returned with two platters of fried pies. Three stacks had a light glaze drizzled over them. One stack had a cream cheese glaze. Some of the filling had seeped through the fork pressed creases and was slightly burned to perfection.

"Talk about southern cooking. Please tell me that at least one of those is peach," Alden begged.

"The tray that I have has a choice of peach *or* lemon. Candace's has apple *or* pear," Dee advised.

"Sit the peach and lemon right here in front of me, young lady."

Everybody laughed at the excitement in his voice. "Trust me, they are all amazing. Way better than the ones you can buy at the store," Aden boastfully assured him.

"I have no doubt about that," Alden replied and grabbed two of each off the tray.

CHAPTER 6

Several lively conversations were going on around the table, while they were enjoying their dessert and coffee. Then Floyd recalled that Mark, Candace, Aden, and Betty had all denied being aware of Alden's complaint. He took a sip of his coffee, and casually inquired, "Was my failure to install you what you needed to talk to me about, Alden?"

Capri squeaked so loud that *everybody,* including Brock, jumped. Sterling put his hand over her mouth, but she kept laughing. Then Aden and Mark started laughing. Before long everybody who attended Grace joined in. That is except Alden. He said, "I accepted my calling thirty years ago. Still, every now and again, I *still* struggle with the old man."

"We all do, Alden," Floyd assured him.

Alden fanned a dismissive hand towards Floyd and continued, "Does anyone sitting at this table have a problem with a pastor using *expressive* language?"

Everybody knew expressive meant foul. They

all chuckled and shook their heads. Brock roared and said, "Express yourself!"

Alden looked at Jared and Floyd and squinted. Then he asked, "What in the godless *HELL!*"

Floyd knew what it was about, or so he thought he did. "Benny. Right?'

"Hell nah! Benny is a saint compared to some of your old members, man."

"What?"

"You heard me."

Jared wasn't surprised that the members of Grace were still acting up. After all, even the Israelites continued to grumble after their *forty-year* wilderness experience. It always amazed him that all of the original complainers had died during that forty-year span, yet the grumbling continued. Not one of them recognized that even during their punishment they hadn't been attacked by a single wild animal. Or that while they were out in the open *valley*, none of the nations, living in the mountains, attacked them. He guessed it was in humanity's nature to never be satisfied. The women safely tucked away on this estate proved that, a few Christmases ago, with their pettiness. It was so bad they literally forgot to cook for the homeless. Thankfully Chef was on it. While everybody was at the church, he did what no one knew he'd always done. Then he'd called the field Watchers to make the deliveries. "What are they doing, Alden?"

"I have an appointment book that I setup in the lobby after church, every Sunday. It's for anyone who needs to meet me and Capri in Galilee the following week."

"The two of you meet with the members together?" Floyd asked.

"Yes. I've been around a long time, and I know that people lie. I also know that women throw themselves at powerful men. Including pastors! Especially if that pastor pastors a megachurch," Antoinette answered. She went on to declare, "I ain't one of those longsuffering first ladies. The ones who put up with women fawning over their husbands, while they silently endure his ego's inability to resist temptation. Nevertheless, I *love* Alden and don't want to kill my children's father. With Capri and Alden both in the meeting, there can be no false accusations, rumors, or double *murders* at Grace Tabernacle."

Everybody at the table laughed. MeiLi and Samantha stood up and gave Antoinette a standing ovation, both wishing they'd had her backbone when they were at Grace. Floyd looked from Antoinette to Alden, and then at Capri. Both women were in their early fifties. Both of them looked *remarkable* for their age. Both women, like Betty Jean, had hung around gangbangers when they were teenagers. Unlike Betty Jean and Antoinette, Capri had not married the gangbanger she hung with. Her parents had cut that short by moving from Texas to North Carolina, to get her away from him. Even so, they were both still *street smart.* "It was your *wife's* idea to have joint meetings."

Alden nodded. He often wondered if Holy selected Capri to be his assistant because of her past. Her being female certainly didn't hurt, but he knew that her gender wasn't the reason. His sister in the ministry, Liz Ballard, had also been on this list of candidates. In the end, he surmised that it was because Capri and Antoinette were cut from the same *brazenly outspoken* cloth. "Anyway, it's always the same ones, week after week. After week!"

"What's their gripe?"

Capri giggled, and immediately prayed, "*Help me, Jesus.*" Then she placed her elbows on the table and covered her face, with both of her hands.

Alden pitched his voice several octaves higher and mimicked, "*I cussed my husband out last week, Pastor.*" - "*Pray for me, Pastor. I ran a stop light.*" - "*I got mad and turned over my neighbor's garbage can. Then I lied and said it wasn't me!*" - "*I lied to get out of jury duty.*"

Tommie grunted. People do what they are going to do all week, knowing all they have to do is confess their sins to the priests. None of them seem to grasp that it isn't the words, but the heart that God listens to. He looked at Sal and smiled. God had certainly heard the abundant flow of Salvador's heart. He was so grateful that he no longer had to pretend that he could absolve them. He shook his head and commiserated, "Don't I remember those days."

Alden knew that Tommie started out as a

priest. He didn't know how the man dealt with that. He glared at Tommie, lowered his voice an octave, and mimicked, *"I watched the playboy channel every night last week."* - *"I fornicated last week, pastor. Three times!"* – Then he had the nerve to smile, man."

Capri squealed, slapped the table, and squeaked out, "That young man said that he scratched that itch not *once,* but he went back for seconds *and* thirds!" Then she held up her fingers and squealed, "One for the *father!* One for the *son-"*

Sterling jumped and his eyes bucked. The two of them had *privately* laughed for days about that boy's confession. Both of them believed that he was just jacking with Alden. Possibly on a bet. Now he was embarrassed that she'd cut up in front of *all* of these ministers. Before she could finish, he slapped his hand over her mouth and shouted, "Capricious!!"

Her eyes were running like crazy and she kept squealing against his palm. He pressed down harder when she inaudibly squealed, "ONE FOR *HOLY!"*

She had everybody laughing, but Alden. He griped, "Son of God! The *fully grown, thirty-three-year-old* Jesus knows I don't *need* to hear their confessions. I do not *want* to either!"

Capri moved Sterling's hand, squealed, and squeaked, "Alden said, *'That's too much **damn** information, boy!'"*

Aden and Mark roared. They at the church when it happened. Capri had almost run into them when she ran out of Galilee. At first they thought that she was crying because, like now, her face was soaking wet. They'd casted their eyes towards the conference room to see what was going on. Floyd had designed it with four glass walls, so that no one could accuse him of misbehaving. They saw Alden jump up and shout at the boy, *'Get your mannish ass out of here! Don't come back in here with that foolishness, boy!'* Capri went down on her knees, holding her side, and squealing. That's when they realized she wasn't crying but laughing. That boy was laughing when he rushed out of the conference room and ran out the side door. Neither of them could decide who had been funnier - Alden, Capri, or that young man. Capri was definitely funnier tonight.

"I don't know what kind of pastors you birds were, but I am not *that* dude! My advice to them is to pray and ask God for forgiveness, in the name of Jesus. Ask HIM for deliverance from *whatever* your weakness is. Then lean on Holy to guide, reproof and correct you."

Jared chuckled and admitted, "They can act like babes in Christ sometimes."

Alden looked at him and nodded. "Many nights I laid in bed thinking about you and Floyd. Wondering how y'all dealt with their *lack* of understanding of what Jesus did on the cross."

Then he looked at Floyd. "Everybody knows that you are methodical when it comes to teaching God's word. So what in God's name happened?"

"They knew better than to try that mess with

me," Floyd said and chuckled. "They are probably gauging your leadership style. Or they could possibly be taking you through an initiation. I am almost positive that's what that young man was doing."

Aden laughed. "You should have told him what my mother told me and my brothers."

It was Jodi's turn to squeal. "My sister told her sons that they would have to swallow their father's pee, to keep their teeny weenies from falling off!"

Everybody burst out laughing, *but* Alden. He was more than a little incensed. "I don't know which offends me more, Floyd. Your laughing or the thought that the members are testing me."

Floyd stopped laughing when he saw that Alden wasn't. "Maybe they wandered in the wilderness too long. Keep in mind that it was the *Board of Trustees* and *deacons* who elected Benny, not the *membership*. Most of them, *like Job*, don't understand why God allowed it to happen to them. Perhaps they need validation from you that they are still in *God's* good graces, Alden. They might need confirmation *and* assurance from *you* that their behavior will not send them back."

Alden was slowly nodding. "I can see your point, Floyd. I was most certainly skittish when God called me. I kept asking, *'Who me? Are you sure? I'm a gangbanger!'* I made a lot of mistakes and kept getting chastised by God. Then I found myself questioning *everything* I did. Did God approve this or was it Satan? Of course the devil kept me in doubt. I had no one to go to because I was not a member of anybody's church. Like John the Baptist, I started out as a *street* minister. Hence, I had to lean and depend on Holy's guidance."

"That's my point, man. Once we've been spanked by the hand of God, we struggle with the smallest of issues, for a season. However, if you are 'not careful, you will find yourself weighed down with *their* sins. That is not what God called you to do, Alden. Jesus took care of that on the cross. You need to remind them that deliverance from our sinful *nature* came from His hanging on the *cross*. Forgiveness for our sinful *acts* came through the shedding of His *blood*."

Jared could not believe the one who'd lied to get out of jury duty. Although a lie, it was not a sin unto *separation*. In fact, none of those Alden had mentioned were. As an ex-pastor to those people, he both advised and cautioned, "Do like I did when I became their pastor, Alden. Explain to them that Galilee is not a *secret closet*, for them to unload their guilt, transgressions, and trespasses on you. Reintroduce them to the difference in moral sins, and sins that are unto death."

"I recommend you set limits and hold steadfast to them," Salvador advised. "If you don't, Floyd is right; you'll be weighted down with their sins. And they will continue to do what they do. Believe me when I tell you, I know what I am talking about. I did that once to Tommie. I confessed to him what I was going to do before I did it." He looked at Tommie and said, "Forgive me, Father, for I am *about* to sin."

"Yeah, and I was burdened *down* with your pre-confession," Tommie griped. "Why should you be weighted down when Jesus's shoulders were built to handle the weight, Alden? Didn't Jesus say, *'Come unto me all who are burdened and heavy laden. And I will give you rest!'* It took me a minute to understand as a priest, I should've told them to read that passage, instead of saying hail Mary's while clutching their rosary."

Alden laughed at Sal *and* Tommie. "I continuously remind them that Grace is not a Catholic church. Galilee is not a confessional, and I am most definitely *not* an *abstinent* priest. Then I say, *"If you don't believe me, ask my sensuously voluptuous wife, Ms. Antionette.'"*

Antionette laughed at her husband. She'd only been a size ten when she met Alden. She'd had a small waist and even smaller breasts. Then bam! The babies started coming and so did the lingering weight. Now she wore a size sixteen with an overflowing cleavage, thanks to her breastfeeding. "I wasn't voluptuous when you married me. It was having all five of your children in less than four years that reshaped this vessel."

He winked at her. In the beginning she'd tried every diet in the book: Water and juice diet, Cabbage diet, Atkins, Weight Watchers, Jenny Craig. None of them worked. In fact, every time she stopped dieting she regained what she'd lost, *plus*. It took a minute for him to convince her that he found the added weight sensuous. But he really - *really* did. He held up his open hands. "True, but you have always fit these hands and arms of mine perfectly, Toni."

"Wait a minute," Jodi said and sat up. "Y'all had five children, in less than four years?"

Antoinette nodded and smiled. "Yes. A set of twin girls, a boy, and then a boy and girl set of twins."

Jodi looked around at her family and frowned. Then she looked at Antoinette, tilted her head, and questioned, "What!"

Everybody followed her lead. "What?"

"Seriously?"

"No joke?"

Brock smiled, propped his elbows on the table, and folded one hand over the other. "We did that too."

"Did what too?"

"Had five children in under four years. And in the *same* order as you and Alden did."

Alden thought that maybe Brock was just messing with them. "You're kidding. Right?"

Brock, Jodi, and everybody at the table slowly shook their heads. That started a whole conversation about giving birth and raising children. Alden and Antoinette had five grown children, and five grandchildren. Capri and Sterling had two grown sons, and two grown daughters, who were 'Spirit' mates. They also had three small grandchildren.

Brock was aware that Capri's daughters were mated to Watchers, under the Ultimate Watcher over the east coast. Both couples had come to the Ball on his island. That was the last time he'd seen his friend. "How are Peliel and Ressa?"

"They live on the mainland, and we very seldom see them. But I'm sure they're fine."

Brock's eyes started to rapidly twirl, like Michael's. It had never happened to him before. Even though he knew what it was about, it was dizzying. He smiled, stilled his eyes, and stood up. "Listen. It is late and we have to get home to our little ones. I will schedule a meeting tomorrow afternoon, regarding our celebrating this Christmas at Grace."

"Be sure to let them know that I will also be installing Alden that day," Floyd announced.

Alden smiled. "Thanks, Floyd. Why don't you install Capri also. That way I'll only have to install Benny and a few others."

"BENNY!! Ah *hell* nah!" Floyd griped. "I've just changed my mind about the entire thing."

"As a *deacon*, man. I'm telling you Benny is a changed man, thanks to *you*."

"Benny is already an ordained deacon."

"I'm aware of that. He feels the need to be re-ordained. He said his heart wasn't right when you ordained him."

"Know the truth. It'll make you free."

Alden laughed and stood up. "We really must

go also. The dinner and the fellowship was superb."

Floyd stood up and walked everybody to the door. He hugged Antoinette and Capri. Then he shook Sterling's and Alden's hands, and promised, "We will get with you after our meeting tomorrow."

"That is unless you want to be in the meeting. After all, it will be a combined effort," Jared injected.

Alden nodded. "I like that idea better."

"Be here at one o'clock. And do not be *late*," Brock instructed.

Alden chuckled. "Sorry about that. We had a flat on the road tonight, and had to call Triple A."

"Next time just call. I could've fixed that flat in seconds," Brock stated and laughed.

"I am going to hold you to that, man."

CHAPTER 7

Brock and Jodi's little ones rushed to their opened arms, the minute they appeared in their suite. "Mommy! Daddy! Y'all home!" Sassy and Lil' H shouted.

He hugged them and then paid their babysitters. "Thank you. We've already fed them dinner," Vee informed him.

"It was good too," Hans praised.

Jodi was grateful they'd already eaten. That meant she wouldn't have to feed them this late. "What did y'all eat?"

"Grilled cheese and tomato soup," Lizzie responded. "Hans ate three bowls of it."

"I said it was good, didn't I!"

Brock and Jodi laughed. Hans liked any food or soups that were *red*. "I appreciate you young ladies. You are indispensable," he complimented, kissed their cheeks, and teleported them home.

While Jodi was talking with the children, he sent a shout out to his peeps, *"I need everybody to meet me in the shelter tomorrow at one o'clock. And bring your children."*

"What's up, Pops?"

"What's going on, Unc?"

"Is something bout to jump off, Dawg?"

"Is something wrong, Wolf?"

"It's still pretty early, we can meet you there now, Seraphiel."

"What's brewing, Old Friend?"

Brock furrowed his brows at that last reply. *"How the hell are you on this link, Sat?"*

"You had your gathering, and I had mine. Mine just happened to be in the spa. I brought some people by who wanted to visit with Kanika, Sonya, Iris, Smooth and Everett. Plus, Sarah also wanted to visit with all of our grandchildren. When I saw the looks on Ev's and Smooth's faces, I eased into their minds. So, tell me, what's brewing?"

Brock was aware that Sat was in his house, and that he had brought *guests* with him. *Their* appearance is what had caused his eyes to twirl. He hadn't seen them in a *minute*. What he *did not* know was that Sat was as nosey as he was. Well, he knew that he kept a Watcher's eye on his descendants that lived on the estate. Hell, the man had even moved in, a while back, so that he and his wife, Sarah could be near them. What he didn't know was that Sat snooped in their minds, like *he* sometimes did. How *rude* was that boy!!

Nevertheless, it gave him another idea. Alden said that he didn't know many in the Watcher world. Now was as good of a time as any. *"You and your guests just meet me in the shelter tomorrow, along with everybody else."*

"You're not coming to the spa tonight?"

"Nope!" he replied and closed the link.

†††

Jodi heard Brock's instructions, because he'd opened the link to all of the adults. That included her. She chuckled and asked, "Why didn't you just tell them, Brock?"

"A little suspense never hurt anybody. Surprise either."

"Yeah well, everybody that was at the dinner knows."

"Damn!" Brock replied and immediately sent out another message, *"Do not go to the spa, and keep y'all's traps shut. Understand?"*

"We already figured that out, Brock. My brothers, Smooth, and Ev are on another link asking if something happened at the dinner," Floyd informed him.

"My boys are going to be up talking in my head all night, Unc," Aden complained.

"The women are hitting Candace up too. They want to know if we're going to have the twelve days of Christmas, or a hayride."

"Don't answer. They'll eventually stop," Jodi suggested.

Hers and Brock's heads both filled with laughter. Then he remembered that nosey Sat was in the house. He immediately blocked their thoughts from that dude, said, *"We need to get the children*

ready for bed. Y'all have a good night," and then
shut the link down.

While they were putting their little ones to
bed, Lil H kept saying, "We can't wait for our
playdate tomorrow, Daddy."

"We sho can't," Sassy agreed. "This is gon'
be the best one ever."

Lizzie and Hans were already in Lizzie's bed,
but Hans shouted, "It sho is!"

Brock and Jodi kissed Lil' H and Sassy's
temples. "Y'all sleep tight."

"We will," Sassy replied.

The minute Brock closed the door, they got
out of their beds, and ran and jumped in *Lizzie's*.

No matter what the daily plans were, Brock
didn't let them interfere with his playdate with his
little ones. Lil' H and Sassy were right. This one
was going to be the best one *ever*. That's why he set
the meeting for one o'clock.

After negotiating with Mother Nature, they
agreed that Fall could show her frigid ass up day
after tomorrow. Frost and Snow would show up
shortly afterward, to play in his yard. Eunice was
already gleeful that she would be shedding her
leaves before long. That meant that his yard was
going to be filled with red, orange, and brown ones.
Man, he hated that crap, but that wouldn't start until
the day after tomorrow. Tomorrow was a day for

outdoor fun. And not just for his brood. He knew that after the meeting everybody would be in a *party* mood. That was good. Real good.

†††

He, Jodi, their children, and grands, got up at six o'clock to go fishing in the creek out back. Even their four oldest and their mates joined them this time around. Jodi, Kwanita, and Maria packed breakfast baskets, so that they could eat before they started. Those women cooked grits, cheesy eggs, bacon, ham, sausage, pancakes, *and* toast. Aurellia brought the paper plates, cups, syrup, and grape jelly. Mordiree brought little bottles of orange juice, apple juice, and two thermoses of coffee. Their mates brought blankets and stools to sit on. He brought the fishing gear, and the buckets for the catch. It felt to him like what humans call 'Father's Day'. And the heavenly hosts knew he was in *seventh heaven*.

†††

"How we going to fish with these?" Lil H asked. "When Grandpa H took us fishing he had long poles with hooks on the end."

"And we had to put wiggly worms on them hooks," BJ added.

"Then the fish ate the worms," Mateo stated.

"And we ate the fish! They was good too," Kenny said and licked his lips.

All of the Watchers laughed at them, but the women, Deuce and Abe were curious. That's because Brock had not brought rods and reels. He brought *nets*. He wanted to share what it was like in his day with his little ones. "This is how we used to fish when I was a boy," he explained.

"How could you fish back then, Daddy?" Sassy questioned. "You said that y'all couldn't go out in the sun."

"That's right," Hannah agreed.

Lizzie knew how they were able to do it. That's because she'd been visiting the past in her mind for *years*. "They fished at *night*."

"At night?" Abe asked.

"Back in those days, night was the only time anybody fished," Yomiel explained.

"Why, Daddy?" Ahyoka asked.

"Because the fish stayed at the bottom of the lake until the sun went down."

"Why?"

"Because the water at the top was too hot during the day," he explained.

Lil' H sat down between Brock's legs. "How it get too hot, Daddy?"

"Remember how hot it was when we went to Africa?"

"Yes! I liked going there on vacation, but I don't want to live there, because it was way *too* hot. I like it here, especially when you let it snow for me." All of the children nodded.

Brock looked side eyed at Jodi. That woman was nodding and smiling. Kobabiel told him that Lil' H was going to be her son. His friend had not lied, because Lil' H loved snow as much as his mother. He rubbed his waist and explained, "It is like that all over that region. The sun beams down and the water on top gets too hot. So, the fish don't come to the surface for oxygen until night or just before dawn, when the water has cooled down."

"And that's when y'all casted your nets out to catch them?" Adam asked. He'd been just as curious as the women and children. He was just too shame to ask, especially seeing that Ms. Elizabeth evidently already knew.

"That's how we did it, because rods and reels weren't invented until I was close to three thousand years old. Even then, there were only small groups of people who had access to them. Mainly in Egypt and China," Brock replied. Then he held Lil H's hand in his and slung the net sideways. The net hit the water and sank. After a few seconds, he told Lil' H, "Pull, son!"

Lil' H did and stood up when he felt a tug. "I got one, Daddy! I got one!"

Brock laughed at his excitement. "Keep pulling, son."

All of the children wanted to throw their own nets. "My turn!" "My turn, Daddy!" they all shouted.

With the help of their fathers they tossed their nets into the creek. Akibeel shook his head and griped when Mateo caught one right away. "Now why didn't Amazarak and Emim know this, Pops? I swear Demons have always been stupid! And they made me stupid too! Did you know back then, Yommy?"

Yomiel shook his head. "Not at first. Many times I waded in shallow water and caught them with my hands."

"You could catch them with your hands? Damn! Demons are *real* stupid!"

"That's how E-du-di used to catch them when we were growing up," Kwanita injected.

Jodi laughed. "E-du-di would be in the water. Daddy would be on the banks with rod and reel. One time Daddy thought that he'd caught a big one-"

"He *had,*" Kwanita interupted. "It just happened to be E-du-di's pant leg."

They all burst out laughing when Jodi told them, "Daddy yanked so hard, E-du-di fell face first in the water."

"E-du-di came out of that water gunning for Uncle H," Kwanita squeaked.

"We'd never seen Daddy run from anybody, but he dropped his pole and took off."

Brock roared when he gleaned the scene from Jodi's mind. "Oh my God!"

"So when did you find out about the nets, Doc?" Maria asked.

"It wasn't until I was on the run from Turiel that I spotted men fishing at night with them. I told them that I wanted to learn how. One gave me his extra net. After that, I hid out at various water sources, and fished *every night*. I ate what I could, and then gave the rest to the homeless widows and their children."

Deuce patted his back affectionately, and said, "Man, I don't know how in the world you thought you were a *Demon*."

"Turiel, and my other Demon brothers, convinced me that I was a Demon, because I'd *killed* my mother. None of them called me Yomiel, not even their Demon friends. They *all* called me *The Murderer*. And I answered, even though I knew it wasn't my name."

Akibeel's eyes teared. "I didn't know that, Yommy."

Aurellia frowned. Turiel was the Demon that kidnapped her. She could still see his teeth. She shook her head because them calling her brother *The Murderer* didn't make sense. "They killed their mothers *too*."

"Yeah, but I didn't know that at first. When I questioned them about it, they beat me. But they never called me *The Murderer* again."

They continued the conversation, while helping their children catch loads of Bluegills. The little ones were excited, and they proudly boasted about how many they'd personally caught. Only the adults knew that Brock had put the Bluegill in the creek, because they were too far north for Bluegills to be there. Plus, the creek was Brock *made,* and it didn't connect with any other waterway. That meant there was no way for *any* type of fish to swim down into it.

The adults were having the best time. They

decided they were going to do something as a family every morning. Brock was okay with it because their children would be grown in a minute. But for now...

"Let's pack it up. We all smell like fish and need to get showered before the meeting."

Lil' H reached for Brock's hand and declared, "This was the best day *ever!*"

Sassy grabbed his other hand and asked, "But what we gon' do with our fish, Daddy."

Brock squeezed both of their hands. Then he picked them up and kissed their cheeks. He really had wanted more children. Nevertheless, he declared he was still a blessed man with the ones he had. He did not want this playdate to end. And it didn't have to. "We'll put them on ice, until after our meeting. Then we'll get Mommy, Kwanita, and Maria, to cook them in our suite. We'll watch a few movies. How about that?"

All of his children, the *grown* and *little* ones, liked that idea. They nodded and smiled. He teleported everybody to their own suites.

CHAPTER 8

Brock and his family were on their way to the basement for the meeting. They paused on the first-floor landing, when they noticed the ministers and their spouses greeting Alden and his group at the door. He knew they'd done it as a group to keep the others from questioning them, and he *really* liked that. He greeted them as he, Jodi and their brood descended the stairs, "Good afternoon everybody."

Their guests looked up and smiled. "Hey, Brock."

Antionette noticed Lizzie, Hans, Lil' H and Sassy. "Oh my goodness! Your children are so cute, Jodi." Then she hitched her breath when they all smiled. "Would you get a load of those dimples, Alden."

Sassy huffed. "I ain't got no dimples, but I'm still the cutest."

Everybody burst out laughing. Capri was in as much awe as Antionette. She squatted down in front of Sassy and said, "I remember you. You were doing an Indian dance at the church."

Sassy wrapped her arm around Capri's

shoulder and pointed at her niece. "Ahyoka and I were dancing, but I was the cutest then too."

Ahyoka wrapped her arm around Capri's other shoulder and retorted, "Sassy needs glasses."

Capri squealed. "You are *both* beautiful little girls."

"You said that you had five children in under four years. Where's the fifth one?" Alden asked.

"I'm him," Adam informed them.

"You're a grown man!"

"Yes, sir, but I can be whatever age I want to be. I wanted to be grown. So here I am," Adam answered.

Their guests' eyes damn near popped out of their sockets. "Say what. I don't believe you," Sterling rebuked and then challenged, "Show me."

Adam, Akibeel, and Doc morphed to old men, teenage boys, and back. Then Doc said, "Watchers can be whatever age they want to be, at any given moment. That's why even though Pops, Akibeel, and I are all over five thousand years old we don't look it. And Adam in real time is only *nine*. He was too damn mannish to stay a baby."

Mordiree hit him. "I'm glad he didn't stay a baby. Otherwise, I'd still be single, and we wouldn't have Kenny."

Doc laughed and agreed, "True that!"

"I knew that Archangels were basically ageless," Capri stated. She'd been around them for years. They'd even stopped her and her family that lived on Hatteras Island from aging. "I didn't know

Watchers could decide what age they wanted to be also."

Brock and Jodi laughed. Then he took a moment to introduce their guests to all of his children and grandchildren. After the brief handshakes and hellos, he looked at Floyd and Brown and smiled. He could not wait to see their faces once they entered the shelter. "Y'all come on before we're late for the meeting."

†††

He had no idea that his request for a meeting would unnerve everybody, to this degree. It didn't help that Sat and a few others were there. They were all nervously holding their children when he and Jodi walked in with their children and grandchildren along with the ministers, their families, and their guests. He chuckled and spoke, "Good morning."

"Good morning," they all greeted.

"What the hell's going on, Seraphiel," H barked.

"Just chill for another moment, H," Brock insisted.

Floyd was about to speak but noticed Sat sitting with a group of men and women, at the back. His eyes watered and he mumbled, "Oh my sweet Lord! I have not seen you guys since *Skippy* was a pup!"

†††

Blake, Marius, John, and Ernest stood up and bear hugged Floyd. They hadn't seen him in over thirty years and were as overwhelmed as he was. "It has been a while, man," Ernest acknowledged and hugged him tighter.

Brown couldn't believe his eyes. They'd all thought that they were invincible back in the day. Floyd had been *his* hero, but Darious had been these birds'. That is with the exception of Ernest. Smooth had owned that man's heart. Blake, Marius, and John had destroyed their bodies to keep Darious safe. His heart raced, and his bottom lip quivered when he saw that they weren't crippled anymore. It reminded him of how Akibeel had healed Betty Jean. He'd like to know how that happened. He hugged them and said, "It sho is good to see you guys again."

Betty Jean and MeiLi were crying, while hugging Elaine, Suzette, and Myra. "I cannot believe Sherell kept this from us, MeiLi," Betty Jean grumbled.

"I couldn't tell you, Betty," Sherell defended.

MeiLi shook her head. They had been through so much, back in the day, while patiently waiting for their men to grow up. She was glad that they'd hung in there, like she and Betty Jean had. "Y'all have to come to the house, after this meeting. We've got a lot of catching up to do."

"We planned on it, Mei," Myra informed her.

Floyd really was beside himself, to the point of tears. They'd all gone on with their lives, only periodically glancing back in their minds. Still, the memories of their foolish days were, and would always be, precious. None of them looked any worse for wear. "The last I heard, you guys had moved to the west coast for health reasons."

"We had," Blake confirmed. "Then Darious brought our *grandfather* to visit us."

"He healed us, Floyd," John boasted.

Floyd finally hugged Darious. "What?"

Darious hugged him and patted his back. "I found out shortly after I retired that they are related to Sat, like you and your brothers. I didn't even have to ask Sat to fix them up. He insisted on it, and he did after we returned from that awful cruise. Then he moved them and their wives back to *my* estate."

Brown was as offended as Floyd by that last statement. "What the hell! That's been years, man!"

Darious hugged him and explained, "I know. I'd really missed my brothers, and I wanted them to myself for a while. I told no one about them moving back to Chicago. Not even Smooth or Ev."

Smooth and Ev were standing in the aisle with them. They had been highly offended when they found out last night. "All of this time we thought Darious hadn't moved out here with us because he killed that Demon," Ev griped.

"Come to find out, he deliberately kept them from us," Smooth complained. "I think he took his role as my replacement *too* damn far." Then he looked at Ernest and warned, "We're going to talk after this meeting."

Ernest chuckled. "Deal."

Darious and his brothers thumped their fists

over their hearts. They all knew that out of *sight* did not mean out of *mind*. Neither physical aches, pain, nor age had diminished the memories of the way they were. For over thirty years fond memories was all they had. They'd often nostalgically tripped down memory lane. They often talked about the fact that Smooth, with Ev's help had brought them all together and forged their bond.

None of them had been surprised when Smooth tagged Darious to replace him. It made sense because Darious, being the oldest, had been the *nucleus* all along. He'd ordered *their* steps when they were *children*. He'd ordered their steps in *Nam*. He'd ordered their steps when they were *spies*. Even Smooth and Ev knew how far they could go with Darious, especially after Darious angrily challenged Smooth to a *duel*. Their no kill brother had been, all bets off, *pissed* that day.

He was the only person that they knew who was both introverted *and* extroverted. If he didn't know you, he was introverted. If he knew you, he was as extroverted as it got. His spot in Chicago had been their gathering hole almost *every* weekend, for years. And back then they'd partied all night long. Still…

"Maybe so, but to us you will always be the *original* 'Commander and Chief' of the new and improved Black Stone Rangers," Blake assured him.

Darious howled and said, "And Blake will always insist that he's Black!"

All of the Stones roared and started talking

about how Blake kept insisting that he was Creole, back in the day. "Your fool ass even put that crap on your census," Ev teased and laughed.

"That's because I am," Blake insisted.

They laughed even harder. Then Floyd remembered what Darious said. "Hold on a minute. You boys are related to Sat too?"

They nodded. "That makes us cousins," Blake declared.

Neither James nor Greg could believe what they'd learned last night. James shouted from his seat, "Tell them who you are related to, Darious."

"You and Greg," Darious boasted.

Floyd looked from Darious to Greg and back. Then he remembered how Darious had leaped over that second-floor banister, on the cruise ship, to rescue his daughter, Iris. In a James-esq manner, the man had glided downward. And talk about skills. That no kill man shot that Demon straight through the heart, mid descend. Then he landed on his feet, like it was no biggy. He furrowed his brows and asked, "What? You are a *Nazarite*, man?"

Darious chuckled. "Nah. Just the first cousin to them, on Ms. *Delilah's* side."

"Don't matter. Cousin is cousin," James assured him and thumped his chest.

Floyd's mind was reeling from one new-found revelation to another. Darious had never believed in *organized* religion. Yet, Alden had said last night that he was a member. "It offends me that you joined Alden's church, instead of the one on the estate, Darious."

Darious laughed again. "The one on the estate does not need my protection. Grace is sitting out in the open. Sat told us about it being vacant and why it was. He also told us how the Demons had defiled it. I was at the service where you brought the wandering lost sheep back home. In honor of *you*, I chose to protect your *firstborn*, Floyd."

"We all do," Blake added.

John and Marius nodded. "And not just us. A lot of ex Stones have joined, for *your* sake, Preacha," Marius informed him.

Floyd wiped his eyes and looked at his son. "Y'all didn't tell me that?"

Betty was confused. Although she taught new members, she was always in the church services. "Other than Darious, we've never seen them there. Not once."

"Our wives work in the cash office. We are with Stephen Leavy's parking lot ministry," Blake explained.

"There are a lot of cars in the lot and on the streets. *Nice* cars. There's always some crackhead or just plain thief attempting to snatch and grab," Marius informed them.

"As long as I've been there, I've never once seen you guys in morning service. I've seen Stephen but not you guys," Mark stated.

"We don't need to go in the sanctuary because Pastor Alden has '*stone*' speakers on the grounds. We hear the worship services all over the parking lot, while still on our mission," Blake explained. "People even sit in their cars, on the street, to listen."

Floyd arched his brows at Alden. "You didn't tell me that."

Alden had set the speakers in the parking lot to draw passersbys. That was because he had started out as a street minister. Strange as it were, he missed those days. "I would've told you, if you'd called me, Floyd," he snarked. Then he and the Stones burst out laughing.

"Alden is the pastor, but we all know that building is *yours*, Floyd," John clarified.

"The membership is Alden's to shepard, but like you said, *'Grace will forever be your bitter cup.'* Which by the way, that phrase is cool as shit," Ev recalled and complimented. Then he laughed.

"It appears that you will never again have to worry about your firstborn being battered and bruised again, Floyd," Smooth injected.

Floyd looked back and forth at all of them. Then he looked at Alden, and across the room at Sal. He chuckled and mused, "Like I've always said, God will often reach to the *bottom* of the murky, for the *marred* clay."

Everyone in the shelter roared.

Brock looked at the clock on the wall. He allowed them to talk because it really had been a minute. Nevertheless he needed to start the meeting.

He interrupted them. "You guys can finish catching up at Floyd's after this meeting. We really need to move it along. Floyd, you, and Alden, join me up front. The rest of you birds, and ladies, have a seat."

When he reached the row where Dee was sitting, he extended his arm and said, "You come too, Dee."

CHAPTER 9

Just as Brock was about to begin the meeting Ariel, and Erica, teleported in. Ariel knew how he felt about tardiness and was deliberately jacking with him. "Can you not tell time?"

Erica was furious with Ariel because he'd done this on purpose. She'd thought the move away from Kal would put a stop to his pettiness, but he just found another target to agitate. She apologized, "Sorry, Seraphiel," and sat down next to Jodi.

Ariel didn't apologize. Instead, he roared, like a lion. "Of course I can tell time. Less you forget, I was there when Abba restarted it. You, and your beast within, were also there, you just cannot remember," he mocked. "In fact, you were-"

Everyone was startled and jumped when they heard Michael shout, "LION!" Just before he appeared in the room. "DO NOT MAKE ME MUTE YOU, BOY!" he threatened and took a seat on the back row.

Brock hadn't jumped but he was curious as to what Michael didn't want Ariel to reveal. "Sit down

---

so we can get this meeting going."

Eric and Libby appeared a moment later and Eric immediately apologized, "I am sorry, Brock." Then he glared at Ariel. "That fool set all of our clocks back to make us late too."

"Archangel or not, you play too damn much, boy," Brock accused.

Alden leaned over and asked Floyd, "Archangel?"

Floyd nodded. "That's Ariel. The *Lion* of God. That young lady is his 'Sanctioned' mate, Erica George. They run a school in the city."

"Get outta dodge!"

Ariel chuckled and then went straight to Elizabeth and slapped her five. "Hey, *niece.*"

Elizabeth smiled, stood up, and hugged him. He was her favorite uncle. They often sparred in her sleep. She beat him every time, but he kept coming back for more. "Hi, Uncle Ariel."

"Would you please get away from my baby, Ariel!" Brock growled.

"Nope!" Ariel replied and took a seat next to her.

Michael's eyes were rapidly twirling. Then just as Ariel went to whisper something to Lizzie, his chair collapsed and down he went. Everyone sharply inhaled. He chuckled, got up and sat in the chair on the other side of her. It collapsed too. He sucked on his bottom lip and said, "Funny, nephew."

Brock reared back and howled. "That's not

me. That's your big brother. It appears that he doesn't want you corrupting his granddaughter, either."

Ariel looked to the back of the room at Michael. "That's you doing that, Mike-Mike?"

Michael's eyes never stopped twirling when he ordered, "Sit on the other side of the room, Lion. Away from *all* of the children."

Ariel chuckled. Then he noticed Capri. "Can I sit next to my old friend, Capricious?"

Michael nodded once. "Be quick about it. Your antics have delayed my son's meeting long enough."

"Tell him, Michael," Arak encouraged. He and his brothers were all losing patience with Ariel.

Capri laughed, stood up, hugged him, and accused, "You still ain't got no *do right* in you."

"Aw, you know me, girl. I ain't got no middle ground. I'm either playing around or warring," he reminded her.

†††

Brock finally started the meeting. "I'm sure everybody remembers Pastor Alden."

"Yes," everyone confirmed and spoke.

"He and his wife, Antionette, along with his co-pastor, Capri and her husband, feed their members, who have no family, every Christmas Day. They serve them at the church, so that they are not alone on the holiday."

"How awesome is that," Velicia injected.

Then she squeezed Maurice's hand. "Before moving out here and meeting Mine, I spent a lot of Christmases alone."

"A lot of us did," Candace injected.

"They also feed the homeless. I would like us to partner with them this year. We will pass out flyers and even transport them to the church."

"Santa Maria and I are in, Pops," Akibeel readily agreed.

"I assume that Dee has agreed to do the cooking," Leevearne stated.

"Yes, ma'am, she has."

"We'll help you, Dee," Lillian offered.

Brock's jaw dropped. "Ooooh-" He bit his tongue to keep from finishing that sentence with, *'hell nawl!'*

Dee had had a smile on her face. It faded so fast, her jaws looked like she'd just sucked on a lemon. All of the men were vigorously shaking their heads, including Lillian's mate and father. Erica leaned over and asked Jodi, "Can Lillian cook?"

"About as well as Sassy."

Erica laughed and said, "Oh my."

Antionette was sitting between Capri and MeiLi. She asked so those close by could hear, "Can that young lady cook as well as Dee?"

"That woman can't cook as well as my big toe," MeiLi replied just as loudly.

"Why would she volunteer?"

"That's our Lillian," MeiLi replied and chuckled. Then she complimented, "She can't cook, but she can fight her God given *waste disposal* off!"

Capri squealed. "I've never heard *ass* described like that before, MeiLi." Everybody around them laughed.

The 'Spirit' Mates who could cook started to grumble amongst themselves, about how she was going to ruin it. Then they went for Lillian. "Here you go *again*," her sister-in-law Regina griped and elbowed her. "Like the good book says, a leopard can't change its spots."

Lillian chuckled and elbowed her back. They'd long settled their differences. Now, the two of them, Lorraine, and Vivian, were *girls*. "Shut up! I-"

Pia cut her off. "Ain't nobody trying to give those poor people food poisoning."

"Haven't they suffered enough?" Maria asked.

"You need to stay in your zip code, Ms. *Lilia,*" Dawn snarked.

The grumbling got louder and louder, with *everybody* objecting. Then Hope suggested *compassionately*, "Why don't we just let Dee pick her own crew."

"That's a good idea, Hope. Be sure to count me *out*, Dee," Faith said and chuckled.

"Lillian won't be on Dee's crew, and neither will *I*," Symphony advised. Then she graciously defended, "What Lillian meant was she and I are willing to help anyway we can."

"Thank you, Symphony. That's *all* I was saying," Lillian confirmed and elbowed Regina again. Regina laughed.

"That's good to know," Brock said. Then he continued, "Instead of having Christmas services at Redeeming Love, we will fellowship with them at Grace Tabernacle. After which, we will feed them, and the homeless."

"What about those homeless who look forward to us feeding them on Christmas Eve," Akibeel asked.

"We can deliver soup and sandwiches to them Christmas Eve. At the same time let them know about the dinner on Christmas," Chef suggested.

"Since Dee is cooking the big dinner, Chef, Aunt Snow and I will cook the soups," Pia offered.

"We sure will," Snow Anna agreed.

Brock smiled because Chef, Pia, Cutie, *and* Dee, made the best damn soups he'd ever tasted. That is other than his mate, Ms. Jodi. Especially her two-bean chili. She always made a pot of *mild* for their children, and a *fires of hell* pot for the two of them. She'd stubbornly declared years ago that she wasn't cooking for anybody but him and their children. Of course that was after Chef hurt her feelings by barring her from *his* kitchen.

"They will be in for a *treat,* that's for sure," he complimented. "Faith, will you design a flyer. Floyd and I will get with you regarding the wording. Nantan and Addison, will you guys print them out so that we can hand them out, with their meals."

They all nodded and said, "Yes."

Brock finally said, "Now I'll yield this portion of the meeting to Dee."

CHAPTER 10

Dee had *visibly* relaxed after Symphony explained Lillian's offer. She hadn't wanted to reject Lillian's offer because of how Lillian had felt about her in the past. They weren't as close as *she* and Symphony were, but they *were* close. She'd even given Lilian *private* cooking lessons. She'd stood over her and watched her season the food. And Yuck! She almost threw up in her own mouth. The woman just could *not* cook. She decided that Lillian didn't have a *love* for cooking, like she did. She just still had the need to be better than everybody else at *whatever* task.

She took over the meeting. "There will be a lot of committees needed to pull this dinner off, without a hitch. So I need *everybody* on board."

"We're *all* willing to help you, Dee. In *whatever* capacity," her mother Charity assured her.

"We are planning to feed in the area of six hundred people. If we seat twelve to a table that's fifty tables. Many of them haven't sat at a *real* table and fellowshipped with anyone in years. We all know what the Devil does to an idle mind. I want this dinner to be special for them. I want them to feel like, at least once a year, they matter. I want them to feel God's love through *ours*," she informed everybody. Then she opened her notebook and laid out her plan.

†††

"Symphony, I'd like you to organize a committee to decorate the hall with Christmas decorations. That is all *but* mistletoe and Santa Claus."

"Aaaamennnn, sistah!" Alden shouted.

Everybody laughed at him.

"On it," Symphony promised.

Even though Dee was an exceptional cook, she didn't forget when it was just her. She often remembered how lonely she'd been after her Grandpa Gus and Grand Mama Girl died. She thought about all of the Christmases she ate from *styrofoam* carryout plates. "I don't want to serve them on paper plates. Nor do I want plastic tablecloths, or cups. This needs to be special," she further instructed.

"I'm way ahead of you, Dee," Symphony assured her.

"Ditto, Grandpa H, can you guys and your crews act as servers?"

"On it," Ditto agreed.

"We got you covered," H echoed.

She looked at her grandmothers and smiled. They and their sisters-in-law were itching to help.

"Grandma Snow, will you organize a committee to prepare the plates for them to serve?"

"Absolutely," Snow Anna agreed.

"Kanika, will you organize a committee to stand at the dessert table and dish it up?"

"Sure will."

"Naomi, can you form a committee to serve the desserts once it has been dished up?"

"Yes, ma'am," Naomi assured her.

"Hope, can you organize a committee to make sure their glasses and coffee cups never run dry?"

"Sure can."

"Velicia, will you organize a committee to bus the tables? Keep in mind that there will be plenty of food, so please ask if anyone wants seconds. If they do, advise Ditto and his crew. They will bring it to them on *clean* plates."

"Yes, ma'am."

Dee shook her head and stipulated, "But not the women at your house. They, along with their children and the wounded veterans, are to be seated as *guests.*"

Velicia's eyes teared, but she smiled so wide her jaw cracked. X did too. He squeezed his mate, Cheryl's hand and said, "Thank you, Dee."

"You're welcome," Dee replied. Then she continued. "Sonya, will you organize a committee to wash the dishes as they are returned. So that there will always be enough fresh clean plates and cups on hand. Also, to keep the kitchen clean, at all times. That way we won't have much cleaning up to do when it's over."

"Yes," Sonya replied.

"Vee, Lynne, and Regina, will you guys organize a committee of the older *boys and girls* to handle the trash, as needed? And to sweep the floor when everything is over?"

"You know we will," Lynne replied.

"In addition, we have a lot of children. I assume there are a lot of homeless ones also. Which will mean at least twenty or so additional tables. I'd like to set them up in their own section. Mama Amanda, can you organize a committee to look after them, and cleanup any spills."

"For sure."

"I'd like the ministers and their spouses, along with *Grace's* deacons and their spouses, to greet the people at the doors. Direct them to the dining hall, but don't usher them to a specific seat. Make sure they feel welcome in *God's* house, by letting them know they can sit *anywhere* they please. Is that doable, Pastor Alden?"

All of the ministers and their wives were thoughtfully nodding. Alden could not believe how detailed Dee was. He couldn't think of a single stone she'd left unturned. "You'd better know it, young lady. And just so you know, you are rocking this meeting, as well as you did that dinner last night. I *might* have to steal you from Floyd."

Floyd chuckled and said, "Thy shalt *not* steal, or *covet*, Preacher."

Everybody, including Dee laughed. Then she

said, "Uncle Brock, can I get you and all of the Watchers to *sit* with the homeless, and the seniors. *One* at each table. Search their minds to see what they are in need of. Then materialize it, as a nicely wrapped gift?"

"We can pre setup empty gift boxes under a tree in the hall," Symphony injected.

Brock and all of the Watchers roared. "Absolutely," he squeaked out.

"Sarah and I are in on that," Sat insisted.

"Me and Libby also," Eric injected.

"As am I, and *The Lion*, Dee," Michael injected.

"For sure," Ariel readily agreed without barb.

"All of us teenagers can pass them out," Sheila offered.

"How about we just give out gift cards, like we've done before," Kibee suggested.

"That's an even better idea, son," Brock assured him.

Dee smiled because she'd saved the best for last. Unlike the Walker women, these women were willing to assist her by doing the simplest thing. Such as cutting up the veggies, cutting up the cheese, cleaning the greens, or whatever she asked of them. "Finally. Chef, Lorraine, Pia, Robyn, Renee, *and* Dustin, will you guys be on *my* committee?"

The women and Chef nodded. Dustin jumped up out of his chair while repeatedly pumping his fist in the air, and shouting, "Yes! Yes! Yes!"

Chef clapped his hands and laughed. "Our chef in the making has spoken."

Dustin's parents, G and Julia, placed their hands over their hearts and spoke to her mind, *"Thank you, Dee."*

She winked and replied, *"It's important that we support our children's ambitions and dreams."*

Then she said outloud, "Everybody keep in mind that this endeavor is not about *you.* It's about giving back for the many blessings we have *all* been afforded."

The shelter filled with a resounding, "Amen!"

Dee nodded, looked across the room and asked, "Uncle Smooth, will you please come up front and reiterate your spiel?"

Smooth had never been more proud of Dee than he was in this moment. He was sure Gus and Mama Girl were both leaning over the balcony of paradise smiling. He walked up front with Lil' Augustus in tow. Then he called all of the kindergarteners and first graders by name and asked, "You all want to help me and Gus recite our creed?"

They gleefully shouted, "YES!" and ran to the front of the shelter.

"Okay, let's go," he instructed. He was deliberately silent as they recited, "Give and it shall be given unto you. A good measure, pressed down, shaken together, and running over will be poured in your lap. For with the measure you use, it will be measured back to you!"

"Very good. Tell everybody where you guys

got that from?"

They all shouted, "YOU!"

Everybody burst out laughing. Smooth was a Sunday School teacher on the estate. He'd selected this age group because it was important to get them while they were still impressionable. This verse had carried him far in life, and he knew it would them too. He chuckled. "Ok. Where did *I* get it from?"

"Oh! Luke 6:38!"

Everybody came to their feet clapping. Michael's eyes were twirling. The first verse humans normally teach their small children is, 'Jesus wept.' Unfortunately, they do not explain *why* He wept. Most feel like the children are too young to understand. They themselves do not comprehend that it is not about understanding, but rather hiding the word in their hearts. In times of stress, Holy makes all things *clear*. Smooth evidently got it. Of course, Gus had taught that verse to him, when he was not much older than those standing in front of him.

His eyes were completely still when he complimented, "Well done, Sheldon." Then he stood up and loudly quoted with a twist, "Train up your children in the manner in which you *want* them to live. And when they get *older*, they will *not depart* from it." Then he vanished.

When everyone sat back down, Dee said, "So, please have a willing heart when asked by *whomever* to work on their committee. If by chance anyone is not asked to be on a group, please let me know. I will find *something* for you to do."

"What time will dinner be served?" Erica asked.

"Right after I install Alden and Capri," Floyd answered.

"What time is that?"

Floyd looked at Alden. Alden said, "We usually have Christmas services at ten o'clock, and lunch immediately after."

"So let's say around noon."

"I need everybody on a committee at the church by nine," Dee instructed.

Everyone nodded.

†††

Brock stood up. "If there's nothing else, this meeting is adjourned." Then he chuckled and said, "Oh, by the way. If I were you guys, I'd turn my heat up tonight."

"You're lifting the shield, Seraphiel?" H asked.

"At exactly midnight."

Alden looked at Floyd and asked, "What does that mean?"

"Haven't you noticed the difference in the temperature in the city and out here?"

"Yeah. I just assumed it was because you guys were so far south."

"We're not that far out, man. Brock has a shield up around the estate and the preserves. It keeps the cold and snow out."

Alden's head jerked and he shouted, "Get the *hell* out!" Then he apologized, "Sorry everybody. I still struggle with the old man."

Everybody laughed.

Lil' H was so excited, he ran behind the desk to Brock. "You gon' let it snow for me, Daddy?"

Brock shook his head when he heard Jodi giggle. He swore this boy was her son. Right down to those adorable dimples. He picked him up, kissed his dimple and said, "Not for another week, son. But the leaves will start falling in a day or so."

Lil' H hugged him. "Thank you, Daddy."

Brock looked over Lil' H's shoulder at the crowd, and warned, "According to Mother Nature, Fall is pissed because I didn't let her in, in November. She and Winter are coming for us as soon as I lift the shield. *So*, I suggest you guys enjoy the remainder of this nice warm day *outside*. Don't worry about hanging Christmas lights, I have already hung them on the estate, and throughout the subdivision."

"I ain't even going to *ask* what you mean," Alden voiced.

Brock chuckled and vanished with his *entire* family.

CHAPTER 11

Antionette noticed that no one was in a hurry to leave. They were making their way to the chairs of various committees. She assumed it was to volunteer their service, *before* being asked. She absolutely *loved* their enthusiasm. It was too bad that none of them belonged to Grace. She whispered to Capri, "I'm going to have to take that crown back from Dee. Look at all of these gorgeous women. She's got some real competition in this crowd."

Capri squealed. Antionette chuckled and suggested to her, and MeiLi, "Let's go talk with the other ministers' wives. I have an idea on how we can all be uniformly dressed."

"Okay," MeiLi agreed.

Capri agreed and then hugged Ariel and teased, "Behave while I'm gone! *And* stay away from those children, Lion."

He kissed her cheek and whispered to her mind, *"Let me clue you in on a secret."*

"What?"

"Lil' Lizzie and I have been sparring all while this meeting has been going on." Then he stepped

aside so that they could get past him.

Capri squeaked out, *"I swear, you ain't got no do right in you! But why Lizzie?"* and stepped into the aisle.

"She beat me up a couple of years ago."

Capri was so startled, she tripped over her own feet. *"What?"*

"I kid you not. That oldest little girl of Seraphiel's looks innocent, but she is powerful. I've been trying to beat her ever since. I can't."

"Tell me why she beat you up, in the first place, Ariel."

"We'll talk about it later."

"Alright."

As Capri, MeiLi, and Antionette were making their way across the church, she noticed Erica was making her way down the aisle. She assumed that was why Ariel had suddenly cut their conversation short. "Y'all go ahead. I want to catch up with my old friend. Just let me know what y'all decide."

"Alright," Antionette agreed. Then she and MeiLi made their way to the other wives.

†††

Capri and Erica were all smiles when they met up in the aisle. "Hey, stranger," they gleefully said at the same time. Then they hugged each other and started chatting up a storm.

"What are you and Ariel doing here?" Capri asked.

"We live in the city. Seraphiel invited us to

participate in this event. He should've known Ariel was going to mess with him because he always does."

Capri laughed. Ariel was a whole *entire* hoot. "I didn't know that you guys had moved here."

"Michael transferred us here, a couple of years ago, to run a shelter for Alter Egos. My parents and brothers moved here too. All except Eric Junior. He and his family live in New Orleans, with Kay and Chamuel." She'd just found out, before this meeting that Capri and Sterling were living in Indiana. "How long have you guys been here?"

Capri knew that Eric Junior was in New Orleans because Pastor Perry lived there. He had informed her that Eric Junior's wife, Jean was his wife, Nancy's daughter. And that they all lived with *her* angel, Cham. She envied them that, big time. But she knew that she would get on Kay's nerves if she lived there. Kay had reminded her years ago, *'Don't get it twisted, Cham is my Angel. Not yours.'* She'd said it and laughed, but she knew that woman was *serious.* She understood where Kay was coming from, because she never allowed another woman to claim her husband was her *any damn thing!* Especially none of those shameless women on the prowl at Grace.

"We moved here a year and a half ago, after Alden selected me to be his assistant pastor. But I wouldn't say we *live* here. At least not on a full-time basis."

"Where do you guys live?"

Sterling walked up and answered Erica's question, "Hatteras Island. Either Jophiel or Raguel teleport Pri back and forth, every day, between here and our home there. Whenever she has to stay overnight, they teleport me here, after I get off work. In those cases, we utilize one of the apartments at the church for visiting ministers."

Erica turned her nose up at that notion. She could not even imagine her and Ariel living in a church, not to mention sleeping in the same bed. Not with her in her skimpy nightgowns, and Ariel in the buff. Not when they sometimes reached for each other, without thought, in the middle of the night. Her mate was way too untamed for that. Thankfully, with him being an Archangel he can teleport them *anywhere,* but Sterling *ain't.*

She lowered her voice just above a whisper and said, "I bet *y'all's* marriage bed is as cold as the artic, in those instances."

Capri squeaked. "Girl, it's so cold, we both sleep in *flannel* pajamas."

Erica laughed. "I *know* y'all do."

Ariel had heard what his mate said outloud *and* in her mind. He walked up sucking on his bottom lip. Then he wrapped his arm around Erica's waist and said, "You know it is, Erica. Married or not, as untamed as I am, even I wouldn't *defile* Abba's house."

"That's the very reason we go home most nights," Sterling explained and chuckled. All these years later, he still couldn't get enough of Pri.

Giving birth to their children had not affected her shape, or her weight by a single pound. Although it wouldn't have mattered if it had. Plus, she was still as cute as she was when they were in high school. She was still as funny and fun too. All these years later, the sound of her laughter still tickled his *heart*.

"Why don't y'all stakeout one of the apartments in our spot," Ariel offered. Even though the teachers were there daily to teach their students, Erica still spent a lot of time alone. As did most of the 'Sanctioned' mates. Libby and Eric were there every day also, and Libby most nights when Eric was out, but they were Erica's parents. She and Capri had been friends since they met, right out of high school. That was the year when Lucifer pulled out all the stops to destroy all of his, and his brothers' 'Sanctioned' mates. "There are seven to choose from."

Erica liked that idea so much, her heart lurched. "They are large three bedrooms, two bath apartments. With huge walk-in closets."

"Living room, dining room, and an office or den," Ariel added. "Plus, each one comes equipped with its own furnished utility room."

"They are all on the top floor, away from the school. There's also a large garden patio, on the roof," Erica enticed. Ariel had done that for her because she'd really missed their private patio in California. It, and the top floor, were blocked off so that the children couldn't sneak up to their living and playing area. Her sisters-in-law stayed from time to time, but no one, other than her and Ariel *lived* in them. "What do y'all say?"

Capri's mouth was literally watering. Erica was right. Their bedroom at the church was as dry as the Sahara Desert. They were even cautious about what they watched on television, for fear one of the actors would curse. Or be nude. They also knew that at one point, a legion of Demons had overtaken the church, including the apartment they were staying in. They weren't afraid, but they didn't want to send them an invitation to return, either.

They'd decided not to find a home of their own because Hatteras Island was their home, and Demon proofed. Their daughters were 'Spirit' mates and lived with their Watcher husbands on the island. They couldn't relocate because they were on Peliel's, the Ultimate Watcher over the mainland's, team. They'd advised their sons to stay their butts on the island, where it was safe. She didn't care what Erica and Ariel's apartment looked like. With Ariel living there it was also Demon free. Still, she asked, "Can we see it today?"

"We can go now, if you guys like," Erica replied.

"We would."

"You need to let your pastor know that you are leaving. Otherwise, he will be looking for you guys when he gets ready to leave."

"Give me a minute," Capri said and then walked away. She walked up to Antionette and whispered in her ear. Antionette nodded, hugged her, and said, "Talk with you later on."

Capri hugged her and walked back over to Ariel and Erica. "Okay. I'm ready if you guys are."

Ariel nodded, and they all vanished.

CHAPTER 12

No one left the shelter but Brock, and his family, and all of the Watchers. The others were meeting in every corner. Everyone knew where they wanted to serve, and so they volunteered before being asked. The heads of the committees agreed that every one of them were a good fit and didn't turn anyone down.

Since Ditto's group wasn't needed until the dinner was ready they decided to have a joint meeting with Symphony's group. Mainly to discuss table placement. Before the meeting got started, he made the mistake of voicing, "I think it's awesome that Pastor Alden selected a woman as his co-pastor."

Lillian was the co-chairperson of Symphony's committee. Although her uncle Floyd was not a chauvinist, he did not have any women in a major role when he was pastor. He did have women in leadership roles at the church, on the estate, but not in the city. She emphatically said so all could hear, "It's about *damn* time Grace came out of the dark ages."

"Will you hush," Symphony scolded.

"She's right though," Regina defended.

Kelly was one of the first to volunteer to be on the decorating team. That's because she'd always decorated Grace for the holidays when she was a member. She challenged Regina, "How do you know if she's right? You weren't a member of Grace. You never even visited her until you married Leroy."

Pia snorted and mocked, "Now, *she* has a point."

Regina smirked at her sister. Then she playfully asked Kelly, "Bet you wondering how I know?"

Ditto's group started singing, "I heard it through the grapevine."

Then the other committees ingratiated themselves in the *conversation*. The main topic of concern was if those old members were accepting of Capri, as their assistant pastor.

"The position of assistant pastor is solely up to the pastor's descretion. My husband and I fasted and prayed about it. Capri was who Holy showed *both* of us. Therefore, accepting or not, they didn't have a *choice*," Antionette answered so everyone could hear.

Then she and MeiLi made their way to Samantha, Gloria, Charity, Betty Jean, and Candace. After a short conversation wherein they shared their ideas, they decided they needed to have a joint meeting with their husbands. They looked around the shelter and saw that they had gathered around the table up front. "How *rude,*" Candace griped.

"You're right. You and I should be in that meeting, instead of us meeting with the wives," Betty insisted.

"I agree. Let's crash their chauvinistic party," Charity suggested.

They laughed at her, but MeiLi agreed. "Let's do it."

"This meeting is for the ministers *and* their spouses. So, Brown should be in it too, shouldn't he," Betty insisted.

"Of course," Antionette agreed.

Betty noticed that Brown was huddled with Smooth, the Stones, and their wives. Since none of them were committee chairs, she assumed they were taking a trip down memory lane. What she wouldn't give to be in on *that* reunion. Although she was saved now, she still had no regrets about the life she'd lived. She walked up and squeezed Brown's hand. "We need you in our meeting."

"Okay, Boop," Brown agreed. He really didn't want to leave though. He was enjoying catching up with his friends, but duty called. He pointed at Darious and insisted, "Don't y'all leave before I get back."

"We won't. Sherell and I plan to spend some time with Kanika, Sonya, Iris and Ezra."

"After their visit, they will join the rest of us

in Shelby's and my backyard. You and Betty Jean come on over, after your meeting," Smooth instructed.

"Tell Floyd and MeiLi to join us," Ev injected.

"Make sure that Sal and Tommie know that they are also welcome to join us," Smooth added.

"We can't leave Jared and the Walker brothers out. One way or another, we all have *shared* memories," Brown reminded them.

"Asked or not, we were always sticking our nose in each other's business," Blake stated.

They all laughed as the memories began to unfold. Those Walker brothers infringed on the Stones territory so that they could cover Floyd's back. Smooth, Darious, and Charles crept across the state line to help Sal, when he went on a killing spree against the mafia. They'd all taken down the Mambas. They'd all also taken a stance, with the Sin City Desciples, when the Klan attempted to march in Gary. H an E were brazen enough to co-write books about their activities. "Talk about the good ole days," Smooth said and chuckled.

Ev thoughtfully squinted. Then he said, "It appears we still cover each other's backs." Then he gave them a visual. "Smooth's house sits between mine and Sal's. Brown's house is on the other side of mine. Tommie's house is on the other side of Sal's. None of us put up a fence between our yards. Five of the Walker brothers' backyards back up to ours. Floyd's, Smittie's, Justin's, James's, and

Greg's sit side-by-side at the far end, with their backyards facing ours. They have fences between their *patios*, but not the *backyards*. That basically makes our backyards a somewhat secure, and perfect, '*u*' shape."

"In other words, a backyard cul-de-sac, for old school gangsters," Darious injected and roared. "Did Brock do that on purpose?"

They hadn't even realized that, but it was a *fact*. "Jared's house is the only one that is across the street. But it's *directly* across the street from Tommie's," Smooth noted. Then he suggested, "Why don't we just gather in all of our backyards?"

"I'll tell the Walkers, James, Greg, and Justin," Ev offered. "Brown, you tell Floyd and the other ministers."

"Good deal," Brown agreed. Then he and Betty walked off.

✝✝✝

When they made it to the front table, the ministers all stood up. "We were wondering if you all were going to join us," Floyd stated.

"Y'all didn't invite us," MeiLi argued.

"We shouldn't have had to, Mei. Dee put us on the same committee. Now come over here and sit down, so we can get started," he insisted and pulled out her chair.

The other ministers followed suit for their wives. None of them expected Dee to join them, seeing that she was the cook as well as the coordinator of the event. They'd just begun to discuss their plans when she walked up with Lil' Gus. "What are you doing here, Dee?" Antionette asked.

"I'm Aden's wife. Is this not a meeting for the ministers and their spouses?"

Aden stood up and pulled a chair out for her. Once she was seated, he sat Lil' Gus on his knee and explained, "We assumed that you would be too busy with your own committee."

"Not too busy to stand by your side."

"As you should be," Floyd agreed. Then he got the meeting started.

Once they came to a consensus, Alden smiled and declared, "This is going to be a glorious celebration. I am truly looking forward to it." Everybody agreed.

Floyd and MeiLi walked Alden and Antionette to their car. Antionette hugged MeiLi and said, "It was so good to see you again."

MeiLi hugged her back and said, "We will have to do this again. Maybe you guys can come over for dinner. Just the four of us."

"I'd like that. And you and Floyd can come to our house."

"It's a date."

Floyd gave Alden his card, with his cell number and said, "Call anytime."

Alden was excited about the plans they'd made. He was extremely grateful that the line of communication between he and his pastor were finally open. They'd even discussed having a convocation at Grace next year, with all of the pastors under Floyd's leadership. Maulsby used to have them, and revivals, every year. Floyd hadn't had either. Yet!! He shook Floyd's hand. "We'll talk soon."

Just as Floyd and MeiLi walked back inside, Brown met them at the door. "We're hanging out in the backyard with the guys."

"Darious?"

"Yes. Smooth said for you and MeiLi to come on over."

"Tell him that we'll be there in a few."

CHAPTER 13

Brock teleported his family to his and Jodi's suite. The children immediately ran to turn the television on. "What movie are we going to watch first, Daddy?" Hans asked.

Abe laughed and mocked, "Not Legion. That's for sure."

Hans rolled her eyes at him and snapped, "Is your name Daddy?"

"NOPE! But Grandpa's isn't either."

"It sho ain't," BJ co-signed.

"Good one, Abe!" Lizzie complimented and slapped him a high five.

All the children started laughing at the look on Hans's face. "My grandpa's name is Syrupiel!" Mateo told her.

The children laughed at the way Mateo pronounced it. "No, it's not! My daddy's name is Seraphiel!" Sassy corrected.

"No, it's not! My daddy said Seraphiel is ugly, and he only comes out when Grandpa is real mad. He say Grandpa's name is Fred," Kenny insisted.

"Grandma Cutie said his name is Wolf," Ahyoka reminded them.

"My daddy got a lot of names. And he always answers to all of them," Lil' H stated.

"True. But I still say 'daddy' ain't one of his names," Abe further mocked.

Doc, Kibee, Aurellia, and Adam, burst out laughing. Still, all of their hearts were grievous. Aurellia bemoaned the fact that she'd had no close siblings or cousins when she was *that age*. Every now and again, Adam regretted he'd never been *that age*. Doc and Kibee recalled how close they were at *that age*. That recall led their minds to the day those Demon brothers of theirs split them up. They silently grunted and went in the kitchen to start cleaning the fish.

Hans's siblings, nieces and nephews were making her mad, especially Abe. "So what! All y'all shut up! I wasn't talking to none of y'all anyway! I was talking to my daddy!" Then she looked around but did not see him. "Where did he go?"

While arguing, none of them realized that Brock had stepped out on his bedroom patio.

†††

Brock was leaning on the railings of his patio, gazing across the scape. His luxurious yard would be reduced to fallen leaves, and bear branches in a few days. The grass would practically turn to hay, just before it died. The blooms on the flowers would wither in defeat, and eventually give up the ghost. El

---

Roi knows he hated death in any form. He didn't know why he agreed to allow Fall to bring her frost bite ass on his property. He looked up at the sky. The end of daylight saving's time, and the planet's rotation, didn't help matters. It was already getting dark earlier and staying dark later. Even though he didn't see darkness, his *yard* did. He spoke to his tree, *"How can you look forward to this mess, Eunice?"*

"I told you that it is the cycle of life, son. I have an abundance of offspring waiting their turn to experience the wonders of living."

"I'm grateful none of my children have to die, so another can be born."

"They had to exit Jodi's womb though."

"But not die! I hate death, Eunice!" he declared again. Then he grunted when he heard that old lady speak to his mind.

"That is not true and you know it, boy!"

"Why are you in my head, Old Lady? I already agreed to allow that frigid offspring of yours to come. Didn't I?"

"Yeah! I came to make sure you haven't changed your mind. Then, when I heard you say that you hated death, I had to speak up."

"I do hate death."

"I wonder how your friend, Sammael, the Archangel of death, feels about that. I'm sure he's now wondering if that is why you no longer have time for him."

Brock flinched at that harsh accusation. It had

been a few years since he and Sammael met up on his island. He knew that Sammael often visited his brothers and their human families. Nevertheless, he held Sammael at bay from his. It wasn't because he feared their touching him. It was because he knew how much his friend hated his job. He knew that the inquisitive children, on his estate, would question Sammael about how it *felt* to snatch a spirit. Those types of questions would over-whelm Sammael, and possibly send him into a deep depression. He grunted, and snapped, *"Get yourself some business. Besides, I speak with Sammael often, Old Lady."*

"Did I hit a nerve, boy?" Mother Nature asked and chuckled.

"No more than you always do. Listen, since I'm allowing Fall on my estate, I want you to make Winter ease off the week of Christmas."

"Why?"

"We are celebrating at Pastor Floyd's old church Christmas morning. I don't want my caravan of vehicles slipping and sliding on their way to the city."

"So you don't care if Cold comes with his father?"

"You know damn well I care, but my mate and Lil' H love Cold. Just tell that son of yours to leave his daughters, Sleet, Rain, Frost and Ice at home that week."

"And if I refuse?"

"Tell Fall I said take a hike! In addition, I will throw up a shield from here to there. I will leave

it up until Spring arrives. Starting a minute from now!"

"*Okay. I'll tell Winter.*"

Brock stood up, stretched, and chuckled. "*I thought you'd see it my way, Old Lady.*"

"*Bye, boy!*"

"*Bye,*" he replied and walked back in his bedroom.

†††

When he walked back in the living room he saw Hans was pouting. When he looked at the television he immediately knew what it was about. Thankfully, he and Jodi had about seven more years to assert their parental control over what she watched. He shook his head and decided that he'd take his own advice. He called Jodi, and his older children to come into the living room. The minute they arrived, he asked, "How would you guys like to have the fish fry out by Eunice, instead of in the apartment?"

Doc smiled and nodded. "Over an open fire, like we had to do back in the day?"

"NOPE! Back then it wasn't really a fry. I personally like mine coated with seasoned cornmeal, and dropped in a pot of hot grease," Brock said and physically cringed. "I'm sorry, son."

Doc knew where Brock's mind had gone. "Why? You ain't talking about putting me in it with them, are you, Pops?"

Brock sighed and shook his head. He didn't

know how Doc could make light of being fried. Not after their Demon brothers had put him in a vat of scalding grease. "No, but I'd like to bring them back and burn them at the stake."

Aurellia shivered. "Please don't, Dad."

Deuce felt his wife tremble at the notion of her father releasing the Demons who'd kidnapped her. He asked, "Can they see us, even though they are trapped in a block of ice?"

"Of course they can."

"You snatched their bones, you put them in ice, and you allow them to see how happy *we all* are," Kibee stated. Then he smiled and added, "It appears to me that you've already gotten a *trifecta* of vengeance on them."

"You fixed it so they can't get out until that great day of judgment. I say let's just enjoy our *good* life now, instead of harping on our *bad* ones, Pops," Doc insisted.

"Doc and Kibee are right. Why don't we just enjoy these last few days of warm weather, Dad," Adam injected.

Brock nodded. Then he teleported his family, and the food, underneath his old tree. The fish, the seasonings, and the canning pot of hot oil were sitting on one of the picnic tables. Buckets of soapy and clear water were on the seats, along with towels. Paper plates, napkins, paper towels, juice, beer, and cups were on another table.

"We need a fire to keep the grease hot," Kwanita reminded him.

"No we don't. Brock will keep it at the right temperature," Jodi countered.

"Sho you right," Brock verified and grabbed a can of beer.

Mordiree turned and stared at him. "But where is the spaghetti Jodi cooked?"

"Oops!" he replied and chuckled. Then the pot of them appeared on the table with the drinks. "It's right over there on the table, Mordiree. You can't see them?"

"Ha! Ha! Ha!" she snarked. "What about the bread."

Brock materialized it.

"What about the ketchup, seafood sauce, and hot sauce?"

Brock materialized it.

"What about -?"

"One more *what about*, and I'm going to make you walk up to the house and get it."

Mordiree laughed and lifted her pointer finger. "I have just one more what about, Pops."

"What is it?"

"My coleslaw," Aurellia answered.

Brock smiled. "I didn't want to bring it out in this heat too soon, Baby Girl. But there you go." It appeared on the table. The bowl it was in was covered, and in a larger bowl of ice.

"This was a great idea, Boo," Jodi stated. "Now our suite won't smell like fish." She always loved fish but hated the smell it left in their suite. Not to mention the grease.

†††

All of the children were excited, because they'd never been allowed to *play* near that old tree. Lil' H, Kenny, Mateo, and BJ were climbing her branches, racing to the top. Sassy and Ahyoka were prancing around the tree, honoring her in dance. Elizabeth, Hannah, and Abe were walking along the edge of the creek talking. "You still mad at me, Hans?" Abe asked.

"No, I'm not mad, but I still don't like you," she teased.

He playfully punched her. "Yes you do!" Then he said, "You know what I miss?"

"What?"

"Adam being a kid, like us. He used to talk to me all the time, but he doesn't do that anymore."

Lizzie frowned. "Adam doesn't talk to you, Abe?" If that were true, she was going to get him.

"Not in my mind, like he used to. He's a grown man now. What we got to talk about?"

Lizzie squealed. "Don't worry, Abe. Hans and I are not going to do what Adam did."

"That's good. I like hanging around y'all too. I like hanging around all of my cousins. The boys and the girls."

Of course the snoop was listening. He chuckled outloud. Then he looked across the yard toward his children filled estate. He smiled when he saw that everyone had taken his advice about enjoying the weather. Chef and Lorraine had the

111

grill fired up with hotdogs, links, and corn on the cob. The young men and their wives were either shooting hoops or playing cards. Vee, Regina, and Lynne were sitting under a tree having a *serious* girl talk. The teenage boys and girls were close by jumping rope. The Watchers and their mates were in the play area with all of the children.

He laughed outloud when he saw where the Walkers were. They all seemed to be surprised at the way their homes were lined up. They even thought he'd had something to do with it. No doubt he'd insisted that the Walkers be closest to the estate, but the others had selected their swath on their own. Nevertheless, it was good! *Real* good!

He spoke to all of their minds, *and* outloud, "Ain't no party like an *old gangster* party."

"What?" Akibeel asked.

"What are you talking about, Boo?" Jodi asked.

Brock kept laughing but allowed them to see what he was seeing. Then he heard the conversation take a sharp turn south. In his opinion, it was *long* overdue. He immediately blocked the sounds so no one else would hear.

CHAPTER 14

Smooth and Shelby often ended their day on their patio. Some nights they enjoyed a glass of wine by candlelight, while they discussed the day's activities at the school. Other nights they reminisced about their easy life on their horse ranch, before she was poisoned. They agreed that they'd made the right decision to move on Brock's estate. Shelby said it was because she didn't feel as isolated, especially with Angel and Vivian around all of the time. Smooth said the main reasons for him was knowing she was safe, and he and Everett were reunited. He just wished Darious would join them.

Most nights they slow danced in the moonlight, while old school jams serenaded them through their wireless Bose *stone* speakers. They kept the volume down, so as to not disturb their neighbors. Or draw their *unwanted* attention. However, that wasn't the case today. Today their speakers were on *full* blast, and the music could be heard from one end of the *courtyard* to the other.

†††

To a backdrop of 60s, 70s, and 80s jams,

various groups were gathered across the grass, and along the walkways. Although different conversations were going on, they all had one common theme. The good ole days!! Every now and again, one would shout out to another group with a question, *"Hey, man, do y'all remember when...?"* Then embellished yack and laughter would fill the air. The different groups eventually merged together and that set off the lively sound of one overtalking another.

The women were sitting on the lawn chairs that their husbands had placed in the courtyard. They laughed at certain stories, but mostly remained quiet, while their husbands reminisced. Shelby, Charity, Samantha, Cora, and Karen were finding out things about their husbands they'd never known. "I think they are trying to outdo each other," Cora said and laughed.

Samantha chuckled and slapped her own leg. "Girl, you know good and well that's what men do when they get together."

Charity nodded and claimed, "Not out do. Out lie! I know my father and his brothers can spend hours telling a story the way they wanted it to end."

"I've *never* known Smooth to do that," Shelby defended.

Betty Jean howled. "You weren't around back then. Trust me, he's lying right along with the rest of them."

"I was there when Sal lost it. Trust me when I tell you that he and Tommie are *not* embellishing,"

Gloria defended. She knew that the men had talked about what happened, but the women didn't have a clue. "One day, I'll tell you guys about my part in that battle."

"Say what?" Leevearne asked.

"It was an all-out war to avenge my baby sister's death, and to protect her *only* son, Geno. Even my mother was in on that battle."

"I gotta hear this," Sasha stated.

"Even Smooth, Darious and Charles were in on the fight in Hammond," Elaine informed them.

"We should have a girls' night out and enlighten all the wives who weren't there, back in the day," Myra suggested.

"When they were more in love with their .357's, and the Stones, than they were with us," Elaine added.

"*And* their brothers," Earlie injected.

"Girl, you ain't never lied," Snow Anna agreed.

"Hell, those Walker brothers still have a bromance with each other," Lucinda snarked.

"Evidently they all do. They are acting like we are not even out here," Suzette stated.

They quieted to see who was going to come up with the next tale. Karen was one of the newer wives, who hadn't been there back in the day. She felt bad for her husband, Ev. That's because most of his memories had taken place through secondhand lenses. Her heart clinched every time he said, *"I heard about that when Smooth or Darious came to visit me. "*

Karen wasn't the only one affected. Smooth's and the six oldest Walker brothers' cheeks would slightly twitch when Ev would say, *"Man, I wish I'd been there."* Then they'd hurriedly change the subject to an event that occurred prior to Ev going to prison. Or one that had happened since they'd moved to the estate. It was not surprising that none of them, not even Everett, brought up the night his life changed. Thankfully, not forever, but for the next thirty-five years anyway.

Nevertheless, it appeared that something or *someone* was going to force them to *deal* with it…

The stereo had been playing one jam after another, in the background. For the most part, their loud voices and laughter drowned it out. Then the song, 'If I coulda, shoulda, woulda,' came across the speakers. It was slightly louder, but not by much. They mentally paused for a moment, but they were able to keep up the conversation. After that song ended, 'Talk about it talk about it', blasted through the speakers. It was so forceful and loud, those who were talking stopped *mid-lie*. Strangely, the song stopped almost as soon as it started. Then the volume went back down, as Gladys Knight softly asked a question, "If we had the chance to do it all over again. Would we?" They tried to continue their less-than-truthful tales, but they all kept stumbling over their words. That is all except Smooth. His entire demeanor had gradually changed from the onslaught of that trio of songs. He walked away from the men and sat down in a chair next to Shelby. She squeezed his hand when she noticed that his eyes had filled with the same old painful *self-condemning* regret.

†††

Darious and Sherell had been visiting with their three daughters, Kanika, Sonya and Iris, at Iris's house. They'd stayed longer than they planned, because their grandson, Ezra, would cry every time Darious tried to put him down. Darious kept promising him that he'd take him to Chicago with them when he and Sherell got ready to leave. Ezra kept holding on and screaming, "No, Poppi! No!"

Thankfully, Iris and her mate, Ashiel, had plans to join the other Watchers for a playdate with their children. Sonya, Kanika, and their mates, Famuel and Kadashiel were going to join them. He calmed down when Ashiel told him that they were going to take him to play with Ev's grandson, Streeter. They all laughed when that knucklehead boy wiggled out of Darious's arms, waved, and said, "Bye-bye, Poppi!" Darious cracked up.

Unlike their spot in Chi-town, it was a nice day on the estate, thanks to Brock's shield. So, Darious and Sherell decided to walk the half mile to Smooth's, instead of letting one of their sons-in-law teleport them there. They didn't hear a sound until they turned the corner. Then they heard, "Everybody's talkin' about the good old days," coming from the speakers.

"What an appropriate song. You know your brothers are in the backyard talking more smack than a little bit," Sherell accused and laughed.

"Wishful thinking or slanted memories is all those old cats have left," Darious defended and chuckled. Then his mind slipped back to a specific day in their past. Wishful thinking, yes. Slanted memories, no! He wrapped his arm around her waist. "If I could do it all over again, I'd confront you and that dude you were hugging on your porch."

"If you could do it over again, you'd still run, Dar!" she teased and burst out laughing.

He went to respond but stopped when he noticed the look on Smooth's face. He grunted and said, "Oh man! That song is a rough one for him." Then he and Sherell joined the crowd.

After speaking to all the men, Darious thumped his chest, and then sat down next to Smooth. "You tight, man?"

Smooth nodded once. "I'm good. Glad you made it."

†††

Floyd and MeiLi had decided to fix sandwiches for everybody, before joining the gathering. They stepped out their back door just as Gladys crooned that stanza, *'If we could do it all over again, would we?'* He almost dropped the tray when he noticed the pained look on Smooth's face. That expression could only be due to one painful memory. He leaned his mouth towards MeiLi's ear, and said, "I have no doubt that Smooth would change at least one moment in time."

MeiLi glanced ahead at Smooth. It was obvious he was pondering something in his mind. "Has he ever said what, Floyd?"

"We've never discussed regrets or do-overs. Or least not with all the cards on the table."

"He's mentally struggling, Floyd. Now is as good of a time as any. Don't you think?"

Floyd nodded and agreed, "I do."

†††

MeiLi spoke to the men, then went and sat with the women. Floyd placed the tray on the table and greeted everybody. Then he said, "That song kind of makes you think, doesn't it."

"Who you telling, man," Smittie said, and grunted.

"So, if you had a chance to do any moment over again, what would that moment be?" he asked. Then he started the conversation off, "I'd be a better father to my *sons*. Those boys deserved much more than either one of them got from me."

"I would be a better father to Lorraine. I also wouldn't have gone in the twin towers," E confessed.

H grunted. "I wouldn't let you go. Not without me. However, if I could do any one thing over again, I wouldn't take Lara to Snow's brother's. In fact, if I could do it all over again, I'd kill him."

"I certainly wouldn't get drunk," Brown admitted. Of course only the Walker brothers understood that comment.

Sal privately thought that he wouldn't let his sweet Darlene get in that car. He didn't say that outloud, because he loved his wife, Charity way more. Plus, he adored Malcom, Medgar, and Martin. No way he wanted a life without them in it. Or their having any mother but Charity. Not to mention his daughter, Dee. Although, he'd never loved his second wife, Maria, he was head over heels for Darlene and Charity, at first sight. He couldn't even imagine how it would work if both women were *alive*. He did have one regret though. "I wouldn't keep Antonio from his mother."

"I wouldn't become a priest," Tommie admitted and chuckled. The men and women burst out laughing.

"I still don't understand how you did that shit," Greg said and laughed. Then he said, "If I could do it all over again, I wouldn't blame all women for what my ex-cow did."

James, Justin, and the Walker brothers roared. "I would not blame my brothers for their mother's treatment of me," Justin stated.

James looked at Lara and smiled. "I would not make fun of my wife's beauty mark."

"You did *what*?" H asked.

"I was only eight, man," James justified.

"I'd pay more attention to what was going on with Hope," Howard confessed.

"Tell me about it! My Mordiree and Dawn certainly wouldn't have those disgusting piercings," Clyde griped.

"I would not come to Indiana to see my mother. And I damn sure would not allow Corina to take Cora," Ev forcefully stated.

"I would ask my daughter-in-law what happened between her and my son," Jared confessed. The thought of his grandsons living on the street, in filth, *still* bothered him.

"I for *damn* sure would not have sex with the deep blue sea," Darious said and chuckled.

"What?" Luther asked.

Floyd and the other Stones roared when Sherell elbowed him. "It's a long story," Floyd said and kept laughing.

Every man in the courtyard confessed what they'd do over, but Smooth. Floyd smiled one sided at him and asked, "What say you, *Commander and Chief?*"

CHAPTER 15

Capri couldn't stop laughing when she saw the name of Erica's school. She clinched her aching side and squealed, "No you didn't let Ariel name your school The Lion's Den."

Erica rolled her eyes upward and said, "He insisted on it, girl. You know my mate has a warped sense of humor."

Ariel chuckled, said, "I'm the *lion*, and this *is* my *den,*" and roared, like a lion.

Sterling was as equally amused as Capri. He was cheezin when he thumped Ariel's upper arm with the back of his hand. "How many brothas have showed up in your yard thinking this was a gentlemen's club?"

"More than we can count," Erica griped.

"They *all* ran away like they were being chased by the hounds of hell," Ariel reported and bellowed.

"No doubt you *were* chasing them, at least in their minds," Capri said and squeaked.

Ariel nodded and kept laughing.

Michael and Verenda had been watching over

the children at the school, while Ariel and Erica went to the meeting. They walked up to them and Verenda spoke to Capri and Sterling, "It is good to see you guys. I didn't realize that you were going to come back here with Erica and Ariel. Otherwise, I would've prepared lunch."

Capri and Sterling hugged her at the same time. "Hey, Verenda. No worries. We came by because they offered to let us stay in one of their apartments when we are in town."

"You guys have not moved here?"

"We decided not to permanently move to Indiana, because Sterling still has *his school* on the island. Plus, our children still live there," Capri explained.

"Jophiel or Raguel teleport Pri back and forth during the week. If she has to stay the night, I join her. Otherwise, they bring me every Sunday," Sterling advised.

"You guys have been renting a hotel all of this time, when you could've stayed at Georgia House?" Verenda asked.

"No. We stay in one of the apartments at the church."

Michael had not been aware that Capri and Sterling traversed back and forth. Or that they were staying at the church when they did stay over. He liked the idea of them moving in one of the apartments. Mainly because Capri was as playful and out of control as the lion. It also put both of them under Ariel's protective watch. "It was kind of you and Erica to offer them a room at the *den,* Lion. Maybe now you will stop *antagonizing* my son, and Eric George."

"You know that is not going to happen, Mike-Mike," Ariel retorted and sucked on his bottom lip.

"Let's take a look at the apartments, and then chat in the garden patio," Erica suggested.

"We'll stay until you guys finish your tour," Verenda assured them.

"Don't leave. Join us on the patio. I've already sent out an invitation to the rest of our brothers, and their mates. Let's have a small gathering to celebrate Capri's position as assistant pastor," Ariel insisted.

Michael liked that idea, because he and Verenda enjoyed hanging around his brothers, and their mates. Unfortunately, with their schedules, they had not all gotten together in a few months. "Very well."

Erica and Ariel led them to the top floor and showed them how to get to the patio. "Come on up after you decide." Then they left them to make their selection privately.

†††

Capri and Sterling took their time going from room to room. All of the outter walls were sunrooms, with one-way view windows. They reminded them of their home on the island. The master bedroom floors were sunken in the middle, with purple and lilac carpeting. The king size beds had four, no less than five-inch thick, wide bedposts.

The master bathroom floors were purple marble, with gold and lilac veins. All of the bathrooms had large glassed-in showers, with purple tile and gold grout. The bathtubs were large walk-down-in jacuzzies. "The Lion loves his purple doesn't he," Sterling mused.

"You know that's the color of his wings," Capri reminded him. "I love every single one of the rooms and can't decide. You choose, Sterling."

Sterling liked all the rooms, but he made the choice, "We'll take the one furthest away from Ariel and Erica's." Then he wrapped his arms around her, and said, "For *obvious* reasons."

Capri palmed his chest, with both of her hands, and squealed. After all of these years she still couldn't believe they were a couple. She'd fallen for him when they were teenagers but he used to make fun of her, like her other school mates. That was because she always talked about the Archangels that saved her, and her friends, when she lived in Houston. She'd told them that her friend, Anita was going to marry the one name Jeremiel. And that the one name Chamuel promised to come to her rescue if she were ever in trouble.

Then the day came when their airplane was about to crash, and Chamuel showed up. A week later two other Archangels saved them, their family, and most of their friends from a Demon attack. Those two went on to marry her twin cousins, Wanda, and Brandi, and were living on Hatteras with them. That's when Dean Sterling realized that she wasn't two credits short of a master's degree after all. That's when everybody believed her, even her doubting Thomas parents.

She wrapped her arms around his neck. "We've been in Indiana for two nights. I can't wait to settle in somewhere *other* than Grace's apartment."

He smiled and kissed her nose. "You are *still* so cute."

"I know, right?"

He chuckled. She knew how cute she was, and not just to him. And while she was confident, she wasn't arrogant. "Let's go up on the roof. They are probably all here."

By the time they made it to the rooftop patio, everyone was there waiting. Verenda had fixed trays of Hors d'oeuvres. Some were raw vegetables with chipotle and buttermilk ranch dipping sauces. Others were an array of fruits and nuts from their garden on the island, along with her homemade cream cheese sauce. Four trays were of various lunch meats, with four different cheeses, and cracked pepper crackers. They all looked good.

"Hey, everybody," they greeted.

Wanda and Brandi stood up and hugged Capri. "Hey, cuz. We know you don't plan on living here, instead of coming home," Wanda stated.

"Of course not. We just needed to get out of

the church's apartment, when we do have to stay in town."

Chamuel and Kay walked over and they both kissed her cheek. "So we hear that you are finally going to be installed."

She smiled. "On Christmas morning." Then she hugged Kay and asked, "Are you guys coming."

"Unless Jesus steps out on the clouds, nothing could keep us away."

Anita pushed them out of the way. Then she put her hands on her hips and declared, "No one could've ever made me believe that *you,* of all people, would end up being a pastor."

Capri squealed, squeezed her tight, and clarified, "*Assistant* pastor."

"That's just semantics, girl. Everybody in Texas is *coming.*"

Capri's eyes watered. "Seriously?"

Jeremiel leaned down and kissed her cheek. "Yes. I'm bringing all of your friends."

"So, how is everything going at the church?" Verenda asked.

Brandi and Wanda sat back down and howled. "Tell her about those hoochies you had to put in check," Wanda insisted.

Verenda knew that some of those women had given MeiLi and Samantha a hard time. However, neither one had said that it was of a sexual nature. She scowled and questioned, "Hoochies? What! What are they up to?"

"Let me fix Sterling's and my plate first. We

haven't eaten since we ate breakfast," Capri insisted.

"I'll fix them," Verenda offered.

"Thank you, Verenda, but I'll do it," Capri insisted. One thing she learned from her mother and aunt was to never let another woman fix her man's plate. Not a *friend!* Not a *female relative!* Nobody, but a *waitress*.

All of the 'Sanctioned' mates got in line and started fixing their mates' plates. Michael walked around and poured everybody a glass of wine. Ariel piped in some holiday music.

†††

"When Sterling and I first arrived, I had to put a couple of those Ecclesiastical heifers in check."

"What is an Ecclesiastical heifer, Capri?" Erica asked.

"A woman who comes to church just to tempt or seduce the ministers, or *any* man trying to live right."

"I did not know that."

"Anyway. They tried it on Sterling, and I put a stop to it."

"My wife wasn't nice about it either," Sterling injected and laughed.

She rolled her eyes at him. "I caught a group of them in the hallway stroking his wavy hair and biceps, while asking if he was Creole. Sterling, being as *dense* as any other man, didn't have a clue that they were coming on to him. I walked up to them and introduced myself, 'I'm **Capricious**,

Brotha Sinclair's wife, and your new assistant pastor. I am saved, sanctified, and filled with the *holy ghost* fire.' Then I balled my fists and said, 'But my hands haven't yet given their life to Christ. They're still straight up out of the hood, and act according to my *name*. Now back y'all asses up off my husband before I lay hands on you!'"

Kay choked on her own hitched breath. "No, you didn't, Capri."

"Yes, I did. The word soon spread that I don't play. Not when it comes to women boldly flirting with Sterling. In church or in the streets, I'm never going to allow any woman to disrespect me to my face. I won't allow Sterling to either."

"To this day, I can't get a hug from any of those women, young or old!" Sterling said and chuckled.

Capri stomped her feet and screeched, "Not even when Pastor Gaines says, *'Hug your neighbor!'*"

The patio went up in roaring screams and laughter. None louder than Ariel. "And you said that I ain't got no do right. I'm going to enjoy having you around, girl."

Erica laughed as hard as everyone else, but it wasn't a laughing matter. She and her sisters-in-law were married to Archangels, who couldn't be tempted by any other woman. Capri was married to a human. She was right to set boundaries with those women. "What did your pastor and his wife say?"

"When they offered me the position, I made a

verbal agreement with his wife, in front of him. If you don't push up on my husband, I promise I won't pay you back by *seducing* yours."

"Capricious!" Cham scolded.

The 'sanctioned' mates screamed. "No, you didn't!" Cha rebuked.

"Hm. Yes, I did, and I meant it too."

Wanda laughed to the point of blowing wine out of her nostrils. She wiped her nose and asked, "What did she say, girl?"

"She came right back at me with, *'I hear you, Capri. However, I am the least of your worries. Just keep in mind that everybody that goes to church ain't saved. If you look out for my husband, I promise you that I will look out for yours.'* We slapped each other a high five and have had each other's backs ever since. That's why Alden and I meet with the members for consultations *together.*"

Zadkiel liked that concept. "Always have a *witness*, Capri."

"There have been too many men falsely accused of something that they did not do," Raguel injected.

"Y'all remember Potiphar's salacious wife falsely accused Joseph of attempted rape," Jophiel reminded them.

"When he was the one who had been sexually assaulted by that ole heifer," Brandi stated.

Michael thought about the memory of escorting her to Sheol. Even on her death bed, she refused to admit that she had lied. Or that she had been the aggressive attempted rapist, *not* young Joseph.

Over time, nothing had changed, where it relates to false accusations. Especially, towards African American men. His eyes stilled when he commanded, "You and Alden keep up the practice of being each other's witness, Capri."

"As long as I am his assistant pastor, I plan to," she assured him.

Michael didn't hear her because what was going on at the estate caught his attention.

CHAPTER 16

Smooth saw how everyone was staring at him, with baited breaths, waiting on him to respond. He squinted at Floyd. "I know that you were in the tight of your life that night. Surrounded by Mambas on every side, without a Stone in sight. I also know *why* you did what you did." He paused and glanced at HE, and then back at Floyd. "You knew that if Cora had been killed, or even slightly harmed, my soldiers and I would've torn Gary to sunder. Stone - by – stone!! That would've resulted in an all-out bloodbath, between the Stones and your brothers."

Floyd nodded. "My brothers were angry that I went in *alone*. They didn't know the ramifications, or what was at stake, because I never shared Stone business with them. I knew that you knew why I couldn't wait on you and the soldiers to get there, Smooth."

"That was *part* of the reason, but *not all*, Floyd. You'd been around me long enough to know that you couldn't slip a grain of sand between H's and my ethos. Hence, you knew if that had happened your brothers would've come for *me*, because I was the *Commander and Chief*. In turn, you knew that I would've been *lying in wait* for them. In the end-" He paused and looked at the Walker brothers. "We'd *all* be dust today."

"True that," H agreed.

Smooth smiled at H but kept talking to Floyd. "Although what you did was *foolish*, I appreciated your forethought, Floyd. It was at that point that I realized you were caught in the middle. I believed that you, although still an active Stone, would've stood with your six brothers." He looked at Ev, shook his head, and sighed. "Even though I *didn't* stand with *mine*."

Ev had always known what Smooth's grapple was. There wasn't a time when he came to visit him in prison that he didn't bring it up. He'd hoped that time and circumstances would blunt his grievance. "By respecting my wishes, you did stand by me, Smooth."

Smooth didn't respond to Ev. Instead he kept talking to Floyd, "That's why I instructed Ev to tell you that you were no longer a Stone. It worked in our favor when Corina moved to Indiana with Cora. I knew you'd watch over her because you damn near died trying to *rescue* her."

Everybody looked from Smooth to Floyd to each other. Every one of them knew that once a Stone, a Stone. Yet Floyd was allowed, ordered even, to step down. "You made an exception for Floyd, because you were not sure you could *trust* him?" John asked.

"I made an exception for Floyd, *and* Brown too. That's because at that point I realized that their *allegiance* was *split*. I knew that the only reason Brown joined was because of his *longstanding* friendship with Floyd. I never once doubted that either one of them would have my back. That was provided the Walker brothers weren't the ones aiming at it. Plus, that preacher had *no business* in the Stones from the beginning. As the youngest brother of the arrogant and self-aggrandized, *'law unto themselves'*, HE, Floyd was the ultimate of ultimate *forbidden* fruit. When he approached me and asked to join the Stones, like Adam, I just *couldn't* resist that *succulent* temptation," he shamelessly admitted and chuckled.

H chortled. "Pissed us off too."

"*That* was the *sweetest* part of it all. I knew every single time you boys crossed the state line and stuck your noses in Stone business. Not to help the Stones, because every one of you knew that we didn't need your help. It was to have *Floyd's* back," Smooth confessed and advised. Then he looked at all of the Walker brothers and asked, "Which one of you brothers would've let Floyd take the rap for my killing someone?" When no one answered, he pushed, "Don't everybody speak up at once."

The Walkers had always felt bad about Ev taking the fall for them. That's why they kept money on his books. "We didn't want Ev to *either*. You *know* that we tried to get him to leave before Gus got there, man," H answered.

"But you didn't answer my *question*, H."

"No, we wouldn't have let Sonny Man take the blame. We would've dragged his butt off that roof, kicking and bucking, if we'd had to," E admitted. "But you already knew that."

"You're right. I did," Smooth admitted and slowly nodded. "The song asked would we do it all over again. Not one of you said, if you could do it all over again, you'd drag *my brother* off that roof, kicking and bucking. Did you? When in fact you could've all been gone before *I* even got there, let alone Gus."

No one responded, even though he was right. The six of them could've changed the damn outcome. It didn't help matters to know that if the tables were turned Smooth would've *never* left Floyd out in the cold. "Damn," H and E both mumbled.

"So here's my answer. If I could do it all over, I would knock Ev out with the butt of my gun and carry him off that roof. If I could do it all over again, Cora would grow up with her father," he declared. Then he paused and looked at Smittie. Back then, Smittie was G.I., government issue. Ev had taken the fall to protect *him,* and his military career. "If I could do it all over again, *Maria* would not be here, man. Neither would most of you Walker boys' children."

"So you've been holding a grudge all of this time?" Smittie asked.

"Yes, but not against any of you Walker

brothers. Against *myself,* because of my own foolish actions," he poignantly confessed. "I should've gotten Everett, Cora and Floyd out, *before* I went for Blue. I didn't because Brown assured me that you guys were on it. Trust me, I know y'all saved his and Cora's lives, and I'm grateful. But I should've gotten him out of Indiana *before* Gus arrived, even if suspicion fell on you boys. Over the years, I've heard you guys boast that Gus never could pin anything on y'all. I'll wager that every one of you boys are smart enough to know the difference between **could** and **would**. Make no mistake about it, Gus was neither a fool, nor incompetent. I'm here to tell you, my old man knew who, what, when and where, as it related to *all* of us."

He paused, gazed at Sal, and chuckled. "That is all accept *you.* You really had Gus believing that you were just a gemologist, and you wanted no part of your father's organization. I had to hip him to the fact that you were the *ghost.*"

"Not the ghost. The *Quiet Storm,*" Salvador corrected.

Smooth turned his gaze to Everett. "Gus knew that you never once shot *to kill.* He knew that my bullets *always* landed in my opponents' *throats.*" His gaze fell on the seven Walker brothers. "*And* he also knew that any bullet y'all fired landed in the *head.* Front, back, or crown."

"He knew that?" Howard questioned.

Smooth nodded and gazed at H and E, and unintentionally smirked. "He knew the difference in a wound caused by a magnum, and one caused by a double barrel shotgun. Be it sawed off or otherwise. As much as he *liked* and respected you Walker brothers, he *loved* me, *and* Ev. He would've taken you guys down in a hot second, to save Ev. He kept hounding me, '*I need a corroborating witness. Just tell the truth, son. Tell the damn truth.*' I foolishly listened to Ev and kept quiet. And I damn near became an alcoholic behind my silence."

Everett had never heard that before. Not once! "Say what?"

"What?" Marius echoed.

Smooth pointed to the left of him. "Ask Darious. He'll tell y'all."

Darious's mind tripped backward. He'd been so worried about Smooth that he talked to his father about it. "I got drunk the day I found out how long Ev's sentence was. I came to, the next morning, to the smell of vomit, and with my head in the toilet. Being a spy, I thought I'd been captured and was being tortured. Even though my head was pounding, I jumped up fighting. It took a minute for me to realize that I was hitting nothing but *drywall*," he reported and chuckled. "That's when I remembered where I was. It was the first and last time I did *that* shit."

All of the men wanted to laugh but didn't. Darious continued, "Smooth got drunk, *night after night*. Cursing himself out for not standing up for his brother. Babbling about how *he* couldn't go on without his *crib-mate* at his side, until he finally passed out."

"His what?" Tommie asked.

"Crib mate?" Sal asked. If Smooth meant what he thought, he certainly understood. He and Tommie had shared a crib too. No way he would've let Tommie take the rap for any damn body. Not back then, and not now!

"Smooth and I have known each other since we were young enough to fight over pacifiers," Ev explained. "We were the only brother each other had. That is until we met Darious."

Darious smiled and nodded. "My father, Harold, considered Smooth and Ev his sons. I told him what was going on. Then I told him that I couldn't do my job, as a spy, and worry about Smooth too. I told him that he only gets drunk at home, but once he was blitzed he always tried to leave. Mostly to go for you Walker brothers. *I* stopped him every time he tried to leave the house in that condition. But what would happen when I was out of town. My ole man stepped up and called Smooth out on it." He chuckled and said, "That old man walked in Smooth's bedroom, without so much as a *wake-up boy*, and clamped his big ass hand down over Smooth's open mouth. Then he poured what seemed like a gallon of water up his nose. Smooth came to jerking, moaning, and trying to get away. To his dismay he couldn't because Dad had a firm grip on his face. He said while continuing to torture him, *'Either you fix the shit, or you live with the shit. Now, get your shit together, or I'll wake you up every morning in this manner, son.'* I swear to God my ole man walked to the door, turned around and threatened the Commander and Chief, *'I'll be back in the morning and every other morning until you put a stop to this shit.'* He only had to waterboard Smooth one more time after that," he reported and roared.

Smooth threw his head back and howled at the memory. He'd been as fond of Darious's father as he was of Miles. And had grieved his death as hard as Darious had. He clapped his hands and confessed, "Two days of that shit, Ole Harold had me afraid to even go to sleep *sober!* When he showed up that third morning I had coffee and breakfast waiting."

Everybody burst out laughing. Those who had been around back then felt a sense of nostalgia. Those who hadn't been around, wished that they had known the man.

"Why have I never heard this story," John asked.

"It was between *me* and *my* brother," Smooth explained.

Blake was offended by Smooth claiming Darious was his brother. He'd known Darious way longer than Smooth had. You didn't get any closer than him and Darious. "He is all of our brother, man."

Smooth had always known the dynamics of their combined and separate relationships. He visualized two circles slightly overlapping. He saw him and Ev in one of the circles, and Blake, John, and Marius in the other. What held the two circles together was the *oldest* brother, Darious, standing in the overlapping section. He came right back at Blake, "And I'm sure the Raven is just as tightlipped about your secrets as he is about mine."

The Shades laughed and admitted, "True that."

Darious chuckled and asserted, "The half will *never* be told."

CHAPTER 17

Although Michael was still at Ariel's and Erica's, he always kept his ear bent towards the estate. In addition, he kept his watchful eyes on his son and his family. He smiled when he noticed everybody was outside enjoying the weather. When he spotted that group in the courtyard, he decided to see what was going on. His eyes rapidly twirled when he realized what the discussion was about. He almost spoke to all of their minds, *"Your ways and thoughts are not YHWH's."*

Humanity, even those who believe in YHWH, just can't embrace that all things work together for their good. Young Joseph knew that. That's why he said, *'What y'all meant for bad, God turned around for my good.'* Little did those people in the courtyard know that every one of them shared young Joseph's testimony.

He remained quiet until Smooth got his gripe out, and finally laughed. Then, he spoke to Floyd's mind, *"It was very insightful of you to force them to talk about it. Now bring it on home for them, Pastor Walker."*

†††

"I'm glad that we were able to express our innermost feelings honestly," Floyd stated to get their attention. Once he got it, he added, "We sit around listening to all of these old school songs. *Memories. If I Could Turn Back The Hands of Time. If I Coulda, Shoulda, Woulda.* As we get older, we castigate *ourselves* for the presumed bad decisions or choices we made in our youth. Then we begin to ponder what if I'd done this, or that? We know that there are forks in the road, in each of our lives. Each fork undoubtedly takes us on a different journey. This situation puts me in the mind of young Joseph. Like Ev, he hadn't done anything wrong either. Had he? Yet he proclaimed what was meant for my bad, turned out for my good. Didn't he?"

He walked over and stood in front of Smooth. "Let's talk about the decision you made, and for argument's sake let's flip it. What would've happened if you *had* taken Ev that night and Gus had come after us Walkers. If, as you said, Gus knew what he knew about us, we would've been the ones to spend a lifetime in jail. As you stated, many of our children wouldn't have been born. All of H's would've been, so Jodi would've still met and married Brock. None of Howard's or mine would've seen the light of day. E's, Clyde's, Smittie's, and Luther's daughters wouldn't have been born either. And although you specifically mentioned Maria, Faith also wouldn't have been born. My mind can't help but immediately jump to our *sons-in-law*, and

Brock's *son.* Doc, Adam, and Ali would've been fine because their mates didn't come from Walker *seed.* But what about Ram, Chaz, Denel, Batman, Arak, and Akibeel. Not to mention Chef. Their search would be in vain, because you took a different fork, and changed the *outcome,* Smooth."

"I hear where you are coming from, Floyd," Jared injected.

Without taking his eyes off Smooth, Floyd haphazardly asked, "Where am I coming from?"

"If it were not for my relationship with you, I never would've met Brock. That means my grandsons would still be unknown to me. And possibly still be homeless. I would've never come to Christ, were it not for your sermon, Floyd. Which means I wouldn't have met my wife, Samantha. And, our son, Carl, would be on death row."

"We all get where you are coming from, Floyd," Luther stated.

Floyd didn't acknowledge Luther. Without taking his eyes off Smooth, he went down the line. "What say you, Betty Jean?"

"If Smooth would've ratted you Walkers out, Brown would've been caught in the crosshairs. That means that I wouldn't have my daughters, Melinda, and Christina. Nor my grandsons, Evan, and Jakobe. Their 'Spirit' mates would be amongst those searching in vain. I'd be crippled because I wouldn't have met Brock and his son, were it not for you Walker brothers," she responded and shouted, "Thank you, Jesus, for *Akibeel!*"

"What you got to say, Sal?"

"Ditto wouldn't have been born. Hence, he wouldn't have been my Geno's friend, and protector, in junior and high school. Geno, Nantan, Destiny, and I would've died when their house blew up, were it not for Brock. I wouldn't know that Adabiel is my grandfather. Most importantly, I wouldn't know my daughter even exists."

"Justin."

"My son, Aden wouldn't have met Sal's daughter, Dee. Our grandson, Lil' Augustus, wouldn't be here."

"I had not even thought about Lil' Gus, Justin," Sal injected.

"Gloria."

"Jackson would still be in prison."

"Cora?"

"My father would've faught to keep me in Chicago. Which means I never would've met, or at least remembered, any of you Walkers," she said and looked across the yard at Greg. "Y'all wouldn't have been there to rescue me the *second time* they came for me. That means I never would've met *you,* and we wouldn't have our son, Streeter."

"Darious?"

Darious lazily hunched. What Floyd was talking about wouldn't have affected him, one way or the other. He would've still known Sherell, Blake, Marius, and John. He would've still known Smooth and Everett. He would've still *married* Sherell. Their daughters would've still been born.

They would've still met their 'Spirit' mates because that part was ordained in the heavens by *God.* Iris would still have had Ezra. "I'm good," he said and chuckled.

"Are you *sure?*" Floyd pushed.

Darious squinted, raised his brows, and testified to his own mind, *"Everything that happened was ordained by God!"* He scrubbed his face, with the palms of his hands, and shook his head. "I would've had to bring Angel's *body* back home to Smooth. And I would've died on that last mission if I hadn't met Brock, and he hadn't introduced me to Sat. That also means that-"

Marius interrupted Darious, "My brothers and I would still be living out west- *"*

Blake chimed in, "Chronically suffering from the damage we did to our bodies, covering Dar."

"None of us would know that not only are we related, but that we are related to James, Greg, *and* Sat," Darious added.

Floyd heard all of them, but he didn't respond or divert his eyes from Smooth. It had taken him years to understand God's divine will is sometimes unpleasant and disheartening. Like his son Mark says it's not about the journey but the final destination. It appeared to him that Smooth had a ways to go in that arena. "That's what would've happened to *my,* and everybody else's, family. If you had *flipped the switch*! Other than having Ev with you, instead of in jail, tell me how it would have affected you and *yours,* Chief."

Smooth also knew where Floyd was going with this line of questioning. He and Shelby had talked about it, in great length, countless times. Even so, his heart lurched at the possibility. He kept his eyes on Floyd but squeezed Shelby's hand. "I would've never met Brock. My wife, my son, and I would *all* be *dead.*"

Floyd's head snapped back, and he arched his brows. "*You'd* be dead?"

Smooth nodded and confessed, "It was my plan to kill myself a minute after Shelby died."

"Then I thank God *He* ordered your steps that night," Floyd replied.

He finally diverted his eyes and walked over to Everett. "It is obvious that what you had to endure is the catalyst for Smooth's regret. So tell us how any other fork in the road would've affected you, Everett?"

"I would've been free as a bird, with an expiration date on my life. I would never cross the Stateline again, since my doing so is what set off the chain of events," he acknowledged. Then he looked across the yard, smiled, and said, "That would mean that I wouldn't ever meet the love of my whole *entire* life, Mrs. Karen Davenport-Streeter. Or be the proud father of not only Cora, but of Lynne, Vee, and Regina."

Floyd smiled one-sided because he knew they all got the picture. He decreed, "The road we chose to travel was rugged and *hard.* In some cases, we've looked back and blamed the arrogance of our youth.

But look at what happened once we arrived. We found out that we are all blood of each other's blood. Elects of God, bone of the same *once rejected* ancient bones. Underneath this soil, that God shaped and molded, our *roots* are connected, Smooth."

Smittie purposely nodded and said, "Amen, Floyd."

Floyd turned all of the way around and looked each and every one in the eye. Then he said, "Instead of bemoaning decisions that we didn't make, we should be celebrating with grace the ones we did make. Because all of what has happened over the last forty years, happened because of the *fork* taken on that roof. Look at where we are living and where our back doors are positioned. Not one of us chose to put up any kind of fence to separate our backyards. Why?" he asked. He paused when the long forgotten about speakers blasted Wilson Pickett crooning, "If you need me, call me." He knew darn well who'd done that. He whispered, *"Thanks, Michael."*

"That wasn't Michael. That was me, boy!" Brock claimed and laughed.

"Indeed it was my nosey son, Seraphiel. Nevertheless, you did good, Floyd," Michael injected.

The men and women started singing along with ole Wilson, because that song put everything in perspective. Smooth and Darious stood up, thumped their chests, and hugged each other. Then they did the same to Ev, and the other Stones. Smooth and H met up mid-ways and gave each other a one-armed hug. The other Walker brothers were doing the same with all of the other men. All while singing, "Don't wait too long. Just pick up your phone. And I'll come running."

The women were quiet but kept wiping their eyes. Then Myra whispered, "Every one of them are remembering how they'd always encroached on each other's turf."

Suzette nodded. "Time and time again-"

Snow Anna cut her off, "When a *real* enemy had their backs up against the wall."

When the song ended, Floyd said, "Now, how about we answer Gladys' question again. If you had the chance to do it all over again. Would you?"

Smooth and H looked at each other. Then they shook their heads and said, "No!"

"Nada!"

"Hell nah!"

"Shit nawl!"

"NOPE!"

Even the women got in on it. Sasha shouted in Russian, "Нет! – *no!*"

MeiLi shouted in Chinese, "Bu – no!"

Then everybody started dancing when the Pointer Sisters started singing, "We are Family."

The music was blasting so loud that it was heard throughout the estate grounds. Before long everybody, young and old, was dancing to old school music, in the *courtyard.*

CHAPTER 18

Two days later, Fall made her frigid way across the estate with a *PMS* vengeance. Not only did she show up, she brought Strong Wind, Cloud, and Rain along. Cloud hovered over the grounds, from the preserves to the creek out back. Strong Wind continuously whistled to let the residents know he was there. He shoved Rain up against the windows, in a *vindictive* manner. The children were all upset because they couldn't play in the leaves. Lil' H complained because, although it was cold, Snow was nowhere to be found. Of course that was because Cloud kept her out. That went on for six days.

Brock had finally had enough. He was in his bedroom looking out across the yard, at Eunice. In just six days her branches were bare. Her offspring fell off of her, but they did not immediately land on the ground. Caught up in Strong Wind and Rain, they twirled in the air like cones, or tornados. *"Are you happy now?"*

"Yes."

"I swear I don't understand you."

"Imagine the weight of having to carry your eight children every single day. Year in and year out. Non-stop, Seraphiel. They want to leave but they can't, because your limbs are akin to an umbilical cord that hasn't been severed. You can't sever the cord because you don't have the tools to do so. You continue to nourish them by allowing them to eat and drink from your body. They are healthy, and seem happy, on the outside. On the inside they grumble and bemoan your not allowing them to move to their next phase. Now imagine, no one can hear their day in and day out complaint except you. Would it not grate on your nerves?"

"Yeah, it would," Brock admitted and actually chuckled. Little did Eunice know, he heard their complaints too. Plus, all the little ones, not just his, were complaining about being stuck in the house. And this was just the sixth day of Fall. Lord help him if that chick keeps acting out.

Eunice laughed. Then she complained, *"However, Strong Wind is hindering my offspring from laying against their grandmother."*

"Their grandmother?"

"Everything on this planet is Mother Earth's offspring. Plants, flowers, beasts of the field, fowl of the air, and the creepy crawling, were all plucked out of her womb by our Creator. She is my grandmother and yours too, Seraphiel! Wood, fabric, glass, plastic, metals and gemstones, all came from humanity mining or harvesting her."

Brock already knew that. Even the estate he

---

lived in came from cut down trees. He didn't mind the cycle of life, so long as that life did not reside on his property. *"So you are unhappy about Strong Wind?"*

"Rain too!"

"What?"

"My leaves were yanked from my branches without being allowed to start their colorful transition. Now, they need to bask in Sun for a few days, so that they can complete the next step. In addition, my branches need Sun to seal the wound left by my offspring's exit."

That was right up his alley. He stepped out on the patio, and arrogantly boasted, *"I can fix that."*

He raised his shield from the ground up. Oval shaped like an egg, it gradually forced Strong Wind, Rain, and Cloud off his property. It kept rising until it was high in the firmament. Like windshield wipers, it oscillated until Cloud cleared out, and Sun's rays beamed through. Then he extended an invitation to Breeze. *"Care to visit my estate?"*

"Yes, I would. My sister, Fall forbid me from coming,"

"Don't worry about that chick. Just come on."

The leaves that were caught up in Strong Wind were now caught by Breeze. She kindly eased them to the ground, and playfully pushed them. He heard them giggling. Or maybe it was Eunice. *"Is that what you had in mind?"*

"Yes. That's much better. Thank you."

†††

Mother Nature appeared on the patio, facing Brock. "We had a deal, boy!"

"I agreed to let Fall in. I never agreed to let Strong Wind in."

"I warned you that Fall was upset, and that she was going to act out."

"You should've warned *her,* not to try me. Now tell that cow that I said if she doesn't get her attitude together her ass is next," he threatened.

"She heard you, loud and clear."

"That's good. That's real good. Now, you'd better caution that frigid cow to take heed, Old Lady."

Mother Nature sighed and vanished.

†††

The children had a ball playing in the leaves, for seven days. None of them came in until Sun rested for the evening. Fall left before the dawning of the eighth day. Not that she wanted to, but because she had no choice. That old man, Winter showed up and pushed her butt out. Brock cared even less for that rigid bastard, but it was what his mate and children wanted. He immediately teleported Onyx, Midnight, and the other horses to his nice warm sunny island. He teleported with them long enough to get them settled. They were happy as all get out, to be in temperatures that hovered around eighty degrees. He wished he could stay with them, but he couldn't. Once he was sure that they were fine, he reappeared in his suite.

Winter brought Frost *and* Freeze with him in the wee hours of the morning. That damn Snow showed her ass up before anybody got out of bed.

Lil' H had gotten up to use the bathroom when he looked out the window and saw the flakes falling. He ran and shook Brock, while pulling the covers and shouting, "It's snowing! It's snowing! Get up, Daddy! It's snowing!"

"I know, son. I'll take you outside when Sun comes up. Now go back to bed."

Lil' H kissed his cheek. "Thank you for my snow, Daddy." Then he crawled over Brock and got in the bed with him and Jodi.

Brock chuckled, threw the covers back, and waited. Less than a minute later Sassy came running in the room. She crawled over him and insisted, "Move over, Big Baby!"

"No! You get on the other side!"

Like always, they started arguing back and forth. Brock shushed them. "Hush! Y'all are going to wake mommy." He lifted them, slid himself over, and lowered one on each side of him. "See how easy that was?" he asked.

Then he thought about something that he'd long noticed about them. He asked, *"Why y'all don't ever talk to each other with your minds? You both know that you can, right?"*

"We know. Eunice will never *shut up* if we

did."

"You the one who talks too much, Big Baby! Always whining like a baby!"

"I do not! See how she talks on and on, Daddy. I don't want that sound in my head!"

Brock roared in their minds, so as to not wake Jodi. They started arguing in their minds, *and* Brock's. He tickled their sides and warned, *"Cut it out and go to sleep. Otherwise, y'all going to be asleep when everybody else is out playing in the snow."*

They immediately hushed, snuggled up to him and went fast asleep.

†††

The children *and* the adults were excited to see Snow. They had a snowball fight on the afternoon of the *eighth* day. Even Brock participated, because it made Lil' H happy. They didn't stop until Sun went down, and Temperature dropped. To Brock's annoyance, Snow kept falling and falling. And so did *Temperature!*

All over the estate the men were shoveling, or snow blowing, the snow off the walks, and driveways, on the *ninth* day. The sons and nephews did their fathers, grandfathers, and uncles front yards. Then the teenage boys put down a trail of blue rock salt, so the ice would melt.

The older men shoveled the snow in their backyards on the *tenth* day. "Let's pile it into various sized heaps and make mound trails for the children to go sledding on," Greg suggested.

"I used to *love* that when we were kids," James reminisced.

"We all did," Smittie injected. "It was a poor man's way of making sure his children enjoyed the little they had."

"We didn't have sleds either. We used the tops to the garbage cans," Ev mused.

"That and cardboard boxes," Brown added and laughed.

As the temperature continued to drop, the mounds froze solid and hardened. On the *eleventh* day, all of the children went sledding in the old school's courtyard. The Watchers stood on the side and, with their minds, pushed the sleds up and down the mounds. The children *and* the adults were having a ball. Even Brock.

Then on the *twelfth* day, Old Man Winter smacked Temperature down to five below zero. That old man arrogantly invited Windchill to attack Temperature. Windchill was all for that. She appeared and pushed Temperature down to minus fifteen below zero. It was so cold even Lil' H and Jodi hated it.

"It's too cold for us to play outside, Daddy," Lil' H whined.

"Didn't you tell me that you liked it cold?"

"Yeah, but not this cold. And the snow is too hard for us to have a snowball fight."

"It sho is," Sassy agreed.

"It'll warm up soon. Play in your playroom in

the basement for now."

"We don't want to play in the basement. We want you to play outside with us, Grandpa," Kenny insisted.

Brock grunted. That was not going to happen. "I'm not going outside, Kenny."

"Can we play in your room?" BJ asked.

"And will you play with us?" Mateo asked.

Brock chuckled and agreed. "Okay."

"I'm going to the basement to play with sissy," Sassy announced.

Elizabeth and Hannah walked out of their room. "We're going to the playroom too," Lizzie informed her.

"C'mon. You can go with us," Hans invited.

She ran over and grabbed both of their hands. "Bye, Daddy!"

"Bye, Sassy Girl."

CHAPTER 19

All of the women, Chef and Dustin were in the kitchen preparing the soups and sandwiches for the homeless. The women were gleefully chatting about the next day's church service. "I'm looking forward to going back to our home church for Christmas," Jodi stated.

"Me too. I always enjoyed celebrating the holiday at Grace," Lara co-signed.

"Symphony and her crew, along with Ditto and his, are there now decorating the hall," MeiLi informed them.

"All of our sons and daughters went with them, except Dustin," Sasha stated.

Lucinda slipped a sandwich in a bag and said, "Ditto said the roads are bad. He said it is even colder in the city than it is here."

"I am so grateful that my mom's and I aren't homeless anymore," Dustin stated. "I wonder how many of them will die out there tonight."

"God only knows," Chef replied.

That knocked the gleefulness right out of all of their hearts. The men had been loading their cars with things to deliver to the homeless. "We have loads of coats and blankets, but I am afraid that won't be enough," Sal bemoaned.

H shook his head. "Not in these sub-zero temperatures."

"Every time I take a box out to my car, my hands literally burn from the cold," Jared added. "And I have on *fur lined* leather gloves."

"It's going to be a rough night out there, for sure," Smittie agreed. "But at least we know that *we* have a warm home to come back to."

The minute he said that, the transformer on the estate crackled. Then they heard a loud boom, and all the lights went *out.* That had not ever happened before. Well it did when Brock lost his mind over Jodi and Aurellia being kidnapped. Nevertheless, they knew it was the ice bearing down on the utility lines this time around. They all heard the children screaming in the basement. They had no doubt that they thought Lucifer was after them.

Jodi shouted, "Brock! Brock!"

†††

Brock was in his suite spending time with Lil' H, BJ, Mateo and Kenny. His grandsons were feeling neglected because he hadn't spent much time with them. They griped that he hadn't pushed their sleds. "Not one time, Grandpa," BJ complained.

He went to laugh at their spoiled butts, but it was cut off by the power going out. He heard the children screaming in the basement, and Jodi shouting for him. *"Be easy, everybody. It's just Ice on the lines."* Then he reached out with his mind, melted Ice, and then restored the transformer. The lights came back on not more than a few seconds later.

"I'll be right back. Y'all keep playing," he told his son and grandsons. Then he stood up, walked in his bedroom, and closed the door.

As cold as it was, he opened the door and walked out on his patio. He looked across the scape and saw a host of icicles hanging from Eunice's branches. He knew damn well that was not what she had in mind. He casted his eyes to his gutters, and the ones on the homes on the grounds. In both instances some of the icicles reached from the roof to the ground. He knew that if he allowed nature to take its course they'd be dangerous projectiles, when Old Man Winter exited. He actually flinched at the very thought of his peeps being hit by them. Especially the little ones. He angrily spoke with his mind so that the boys wouldn't hear, *"I warned you to keep your bad ass kids in check. Didn't I, Old Lady?"*

Mother Nature appeared on the patio. *"You did. What are they doing now, boy?"*

"Look at my damn yard! Look at my tree!"

She looked out at the yard. Her eyes kept going *until* they rolled upon Eunice. That old tree's highest branches were about to snap from the weight of the icicles. She knew that *those* branches represented the *Ultimate* Watchers. The ones just below them represented all of the Watchers that lived on the estate. They were in just as much peril. She knew if even one broke off the boy would lose it. She stretched her arms upwards and shouted, "Come to mama, West Wind. Come quickly."

"Too late! You are not welcome on my property," Brock barked and pushed West Wind back. Then he raised his shield, from the ground up. Not only on the estate, but from Indiana's southern line to the northern line, right up to Lake Michigan. *And* from Indiana's east and west state lines.

Mother Nature panicked. *"You can't do that, boy! You are going to cause massive flooding!"*

"When have you ever known me to half-step, Old Lady?" he asked and planted a scene in her head.

She took a look to see what else he'd done and shook her head. He'd simultaneously dredged *deep* pipelines in every reservoir, in every city in the state. For the smaller cities that didn't have reservoirs, he inserted wider pipes. Those lines flowed to all the closest waterways. Even though the lakes, rivers, and oceans, were frozen on top, they still flowed in their depth. *"This is Winter's season. How warm are you going to make it, boy."*

"I don't give a damn about Winter. He didn't take the homeless into consideration, did he?"

"How warm, boy?"

"You'll find out when everyone else does."

"Everybody will notice that something is not right."

"According to the news there is already major climate changes going on. Is there not? Your children have been acting out all over the world. This will just add to the news coverage. Tell your offspring I said don't come near my property unless I invite them. That goes for you too. Now get off my patio, and my estate, Old Lady!"

She knew that at this point there was no reasoning with him. She sighed, said, *"We'll talk when you calm down,"* and vanished.

He reached out and blasted the icicles off Eunice, and the trees in the preserves. Then he stepped back in his bedroom, closed the patio door, and blasted the ones hanging on all the roofs. The patio was bombarded with *sharp* falling ice. Some spiked the flowers in their pots.

The boys came running through his bedroom door. "What was that, Daddy?"

He eased their spirits and answered, "Old Man Winter's taking a hike."

"Is he taking the snow away too?" BJ asked.

"No, but it will soften up so you little monsters can play in it."

"Tonight?" Kenny asked.

"No. Maybe day after tomorrow."

"Tomorrow is our birthday," Mateo reminded him.

"I know. We'll have cake and ice cream after church. Then a snowball fight the next day."

They ran and jumped on the bed. Then they started bouncing up and down, shouting, "Cake! Ice cream! Snowball fight! Cake! Ice cream! Snowball fight!"

Brock shook his head. "C'mon, let's go to the playroom. Y'all can jump all you want on the trampoline."

†††

Brown, Ev, and Justin had just finished putting the last load in their cars. Seconds after they walked back inside, icicles crashed at the backdoor. They, and everyone in the kitchen, jumped. They turned around to see a mountain of ice blocking the door. Brown rubbed the top of his head and griped, "Well damn! That was *close*."

They'd all experienced falling icicles before. However, it only happened when the weather warmed up. "The temperature must be rising," Ev surmised.

Jodi burst out laughing. "Oh please! Y'all know good and well Brock took one look at those sickles and lost it."

"You're right, Jo," Amanda agreed. "I'll bet all of our yards are covered in them."

"I imagine he knocked them off his old tree, and also the trees in the preserve," Smooth stated and moved towards the back window.

Everyone moved toward the windows facing the tree. Sure enough, piles of ice was laying at Eunice's feet, and her branches were bare. They cracked up laughing.

"Do you guys think it will be safe to take off now?" James asked.

"Yeah. Let's go," H instructed. Then he sent a shout out to Brock, *"We're leaving now. Are you coming?"*

Brock spoke so that everyone could hear him, even his and Doc's Watchers, Ditto's crew, and Symphony's group. *"I'm not going with you birds. I'm staying with the women and children. Both teams are already in the city, with Ditto and his crew. They are on this link and know that you guys are on the way. Shout out if you guys need me."*

"We'll meet all of you guys in the alley on 5th and Monroe," Doc advised. He couldn't wait for them to see what Brock had done this year for the homeless.

"Alright. Talk with you later, Seraphiel," H replied. Then he and the men kissed their wives and walked out the back door.

The women made their way to the spa, the minute the men pulled off.

CHAPTER 20

The caravan of SUVs lined up in the alley, directly behind an old vacant hotel. The Watchers were all smiles when they opened each one of the vehicle's doors. "Hey," they all greeted.

The men looked around and furrowed their brows. "We didn't see anyone on the streets on our way here," H informed them. "There are none in this alley, either."

"We know," Akibeel said and smiled. "We've been out here all evening gathering them up."

"For what?" H asked.

"Where did you guys take them? To a shelter?" Jared asked.

"Nope! We put them up in this eight-story hotel," Akibeel bragged. He was about to burst with joy because this was his mission in life.

"Is that legal?" Smooth asked.

"Why should it matter? The building is just sitting here empty. It may be cold inside, but I guarantee you it's not as cold as it is out here," H argued.

"It's not cold inside, H. Not anymore," Ram

assured him.

H chuckled. "I guess you Watchers did your thing?"

"In a manner of speaking," Chaz said and chuckled.

"What's up, son?" Howard asked.

"Uncle Brock had my wife buy this hotel two weeks ago," Lamar informed them.

Clyde looked at his son and asked, "What did you say?"

"I said, Uncle Brock had Patience buy this hotel two weeks ago, Dad."

Doc laughed at the expression on all of the men's faces. "As soon as Winter started to act up. He knew that no one would be able to survive in twenty-below zero weather. So, he provided them a warm place to stay."

Ariel appeared in the crowd. "Michael, Eric and I wanted in on it. So, we furnished it."

The men were outdone. "How many rooms are there?" James asked.

"Each floor has twenty rooms. Each rooms has two bedrooms, and a bathroom. Ariel and Michael furnished them with new beds, linen, towels, soap, and deodorant. Once we had them in place, I furnished them with clothes, coats, gloves, hats, and boots," Arak bragged.

"That's one hundred and sixty rooms. Three hundred and twenty beds," E calculated.

Akibeel was still smiling. "It's awesome, ain't it!"

"Yeah. But I don't know about men, women and children all staying under the same roof," E voiced. "There's bound to be trouble."

"Eric has assigned Nitsuj to lead a group of Alter Egos who will reside here with them," Ariel advised.

Justin smiled. "My *mother?*"

Ariel nodded. "Yes. Trust me, your mother is as fierce as it gets. That Alter Ego can handle any and all conflicts. None of them know what she is. They will never have a need to know, provided they behave."

"Plus, I'll be here every day," Akibeel informed them.

H looked at Akibeel and smiled. "This is right up your alley, ain't it."

Akibeel almost broke his jaw smiling. "Everything I went through was preparing me for *this* assignment. I know what it is like to be dirty, hungry, and homeless. No matter what my past was, it got me here," he testified and waved his hand. "I hope to encourage all of them with my story."

All of the old schools felt that thang, especially Smooth. It was what they'd grappled with earlier. They looked at Floyd, he smiled and looked at Mark. Mark slapped Akibeel five and said, "It's not about the journey, but the destination."

All of his cousins and the preachers shouted, "Preach, Mark."

"In addition to my being here, I have asked Mama Lula to come once a week and teach a Bible study class."

Jared and Floyd's eyes bulged. They knew that he had an affection for Lula. He'd been sneaking bathroom tissue to her for years. "Mama Lula? You *know* Lula?" Jared asked.

Once again, Akibeel smiled wide enough to show all of his teeth. "She caught me three Christmases ago putting the bathroom tissue on her back porch."

Floyd cut him off. "She saw you *teleport* there?"

He nodded and chuckled. "Yeah. She busted me. She invited me inside to talk. We talked until the sun came up. We've been friends ever since. She wanted to come with us tonight so that she could meet the people. I told her to just wait because I didn't want to expose all of you guys. I will bring her after the dinner at the church tomorrow."

"Does Brock know?" Denel asked.

Akibeel smirked. "You mean my *nosey* Pops?"

They all heard, *"Watch it, boy!"*

Akibeel cracked up laughing. "Yeah, he knows."

"She's never told anyone about you?" Ram asked.

Akibeel shook his head. "She's a saint and would never do anything to *hurt* me. She calls me her son."

"I'd love to be introduced to her," Ali stated.

"We all would," Doc injected.

"I'll introduce her to you guys after church tomorrow."

†††

"So how long will they be allowed to stay in this hotel?" Luther asked. "Some don't want to do better. They have gotten very comfortable with panhandling."

"Those are the ones that ran and filled up the shelters the minute it got cold," Akibeel informed them. "They come out during the day and beg for money, but rush back to the shelter early, so that no one can get their beds. Those *so-called* men don't even consider that they may be in a bed that a child should be in."

"Those that are in *this* hotel can stay until they can find a job and get back on their feet. If they don't want to work, they can only stay through the cold spell," Doc stipulated.

"Some of the women have offered to be the cooks. Others have promised to do their part in keeping the hotel clean. The men have offered to do whatever is needed. Like keeping the yard up, collecting the trash, and washing the windows," Donnell injected.

Arak pointed up towards the neon sign on the hotel that, his mate, Faith had designed. "How do you guys like the name?"

They all looked up and collectively said, "KIBEE'S SHELTERING ARMS."

"Get out!" Balam and Caim said at the same

time. Akibeel was and had always been their boy.

"It's named after *you*, Kibee?" Adam asked.

"Pops insisted on it. He knows my heart and that I have an unyielding need to give back. And not just during the holidays."

"Maybe we can all spend time here."

"You're more than welcome."

They heard Brock's voice again, *"It is my hope that Dustin will become the cook at this hotel."*

Dustin slapped his father, G a high five, hugged him, and shouted, "Yes!"

"You know that means that I will be here sometimes too, Brock," G advised. *"That is until I am sure my son is safe."*

"There is no need for you to be there, G. Akibeel and Nitsuj are more than capable of keeping your boy safe."

They heard Julia impart, *"You have to cut the apron strings, G. This is our son's dream. He does not want 'daddy' going to work with him."*

Everybody looked at him and roared. She chuckled and added, *"Besides, the wounded soldiers still need you at their house."*

"Alright," G agreed.

Brock chuckled. *"By the way, Xathanael, be sure that Zakzakiel, Jaoel and Lahabiel come with you, Gamaliel, Tatrasiel and Orphamiel, tomorrow. Make sure they are prepared to enjoy themselves."*

X knew that Brock knew Z, J and L did not like being around a lot of humans. They wouldn't even come to church services on the estate. They liked hanging around the wounded soldiers because they didn't have to pretend to be what they weren't. Happy!! *"They'll be there. I'll tell them that you said that they don't have a choice."*

"You're right. They don't!"

†††

The men finally went inside the hotel. It did not surprise them that no one was on the first floor. All of them would've went straight to a soft bed too, after sleeping on the hard and cold ground. Nevertheless, Ariel and Michael had also furnished it with nice furniture in the lobby, along with a big screen television. Dustin wanted to see the kitchen first. His eyes glowed as he checked out the commercial sized appliances. It even had a counter, where he could pass the plates out to a waiter, if he had one. "Look at this kitchen, Dad. My life just keeps getting better, ever since you rescued me and Mom," he said and hugged G. Then he whispered to his mind, *"I love you, man. Thank you for being my dad."*

G's eyes watered. He squeezed his son tight. Little did he know, it was him that had been blessed. He squeezed him even tighter and whispered, *"I love you too, son. You and Julia make this battle worth fighting."*

Julia was at the church helping with the decorations, but she heard them. They heard her sob and say, *"I love you both."*

None of them knew that Brock was up to his

old tricks. Snooping! He had to wipe his own eyes. *"Chef will help you pick out your own utensils, and pots and pans, Dustin."*

"I sure will. Day after tomorrow," Chef agreed. *"Every Chef needs to pick out his own tools."*

Dustin pulled away from G and smiled. Talk about being in seventh heaven. All he'd ever wanted was to cook for people. What a way to start. Cooking for the homeless! His voice cracked when he replied, *"Okay."*

That boy was about to make all of the men cry, even Ariel. He immediately asked, "Why don't we set the food up in the dining hall."

"That's a good idea. It'll get them out of their rooms for a few minutes."

The Watchers went from room to room inviting the residents to come downstairs and sit at the table and eat. It surprised Justin that his mother, Nitsuj was in the mix. He'd thought that she'd be there invisibly. *"What are you doing here, Mama?"*

"In order to gain their trust, I have to be one of them, son."

He smiled. *"That was a good plan."*

They all accepted the invite to eat downstairs. Mainly because it had been a long time since most of them had sat at a table. Once down there, they were given the flyers to the church service.

"How will we get there?" one of the ladies asked.

"What is your name?" Doc asked.

"Martha Ruff."

"Good to meet you, Martha. My name is Doc. I will be here tomorrow morning at eight, with a bus to pick up anybody who wants to go."

"Okay. I don't have a comb, or gel, to tighten up my twists. Will they care how my hair looks?"

Dustin came out of the kitchen carrying a bag that G had just produced. "Hello. I am Dustin. I will be y'all's cook, starting day after tomorrow. In the meantime, we brought combs, brushes, shampoo, gels, and hairdryers with us."

All the women reached for it.

"Did you bring any clippers?" one man asked. "I used to be a barber. I'll tighten up all the men's hair."

"There's another bag in the kitchen, son," G told Dustin.

"Oh. I didn't see it," he covered. Then he went in and brought a bag out. "It looks like there are clippers, a lot of electric curlers, a bunch of coconut oil, and oil sheen in this one."

"Alright then."

†††

They left after serving up the soup and sandwiches. They wanted the people in the house to get acquainted with each other. Before they left, H turned the television on in the lobby. He smiled when he found the movie, "This Christmas" on BET. "That'll keep them downstairs for a while."

When they opened their car doors they

remembered the blankets and coats they'd brought. "What should we do with these," Sal asked.

"They surely don't need them now. Not after Arak did his thing," Smittie stated.

They all heard Brock instruct, *"Take them and a few flyers to the women's and men's shelters."*

"Good deal," Floyd responded.

**CELEBRATE
CHRISTMAS
WITH US
AT
GRACE
CHRISTIAN
TABERNACLE**

Services: 10:00am
Dinner: Afterwards

CHAPTER 21

The temperature had climbed to twenty above zero overnight. Although not as cold as the previous day, it was still too cold to melt Snow. The snowplows were out cleaning the major streets, including the one that Grace sat on, but not the side ones. Brock had reached out, the moment he'd spanked Winter's butt, and cleared the church's parking lot.

As was expected, many of the members arrived an hour early. The weather conditions were a factor, but not in totality. It was the fact that Pastor Floyd was finally going to install their pastor. That meant that he was going to bring the word. It was like getting two gifts in one. The early birds also wanted to be sure that they got a seat on the floor, instead of the balcony.

The street was lined with cars and buses, waiting to get into the parking lot. The parking ministry had coned off a lane for the buses, ministers, and the guests from the estate. That allowed them to move on, without pause to their designated parking area. Blake stood on one end of the street, and Marius on the other. Both of them directed vehicles coming, from both directions on which lane to get in. Although the buses were obvious to spot, the cars were not. That was why the caravan from Brock's estate had stickers on their windows that said DINNER COMMITTEE. Whenever any of the two pulled up, they instructed them to the express lane, so to speak.

Once the vehicles pulled into the lot, there was a fork in the cones. Stephen Leavy directed the buses to take the fork that led to the door closest to the front door. He directed the others to drive around to the back of the church.

When Smittie drove up with Floyd, Jared, Tommie and Sal, Stephen beckoned him to roll his window down. Then he spoke, and instructed, "Drive up on the lip of the garage. Someone will meet you there."

"Alright," Smittie agreed. When he turned the corner and saw *who* was waiting he snarked, "You gotta be *kidding* me."

Floyd and Jared chuckled. Smittie looked in his rearview mirror at Jared and rolled his eyes. Jared chortled and said to Smittie's mind, *"The only consistency on this side of the grave is change."*

Smittie grunted. He, Jared, and Desiree's father, William, were all friends in high school. All of them were ho' dogs back then, dating more than one girl at a time. He'd done it because he was in love with both Leevearne and Verenda. Jared and William did it to one up the jocks. Jared had even boasted about doing Verenda. He hadn't believed it, because he'd boasted to a *jock*, not to him *personally*. He still didn't know if he actually had. And he didn't *want* to know.

None of them were into sports, even though they were all well *over* six feet. While he and William joined the chess club, Jared joined the chemistry club. That choice was considered more nerdier than chess. He'd told him back then that there was a dangerous man behind that *Mr. Clean* façade. While he and William went straight to the military, Jared went to college. Then he got hired in the mill as a supervising metallurgical engineer. The man just had an unyielding affinity for chemical compounds and *exact* measurements.

He grunted again and said, *"Not that much change. I understand that you baptized your ex in a new covenant. I heard that you even threatened to baptize that woman in acid next time. I knew that I was right about you, back in the day. The last I checked, still waters still run deep, man."*

Jared was amused at the expression on his face. The only person who *really* knew him back in the day was Smith Walker. Not because he'd seen anything he'd done, but because Smith wasn't fooled by his *pretense*.

Smith used to publicly call him 'Mister Clean', because of the sharp way he dressed. Privately he'd say, 'You ain't fooling me. You got a quiet killer hiding beneath the surface, *King*. I pity the fools who find out the hard way that still waters run deep.' He'd come right back with, 'Just so long as *we* understand each other, *Rufus.*'

He reached over the seat and firmly squeezed Smittie's shoulder. Then he reiterated to his mind, *"Just so we understand each other."*

†††

Benny was waiting for them at the open garage door. He stepped to the passenger side and spoke when Floyd lowered his window. Then he looked across Floyd and instructed, "Pull on into the garage, Brotha Smittie."

Smittie nodded and wordlessly complied. Benny opened Floyd's door the minute Smittie put the car in park. Then he reached for Floyd's Bible and insisted, "Let me carry this for you, Pastor Floyd."

Floyd smiled and handed him the Bible. "Thank you, Brotha Benny."

When they were all out of the car, Benny informed them, "Alden is waiting for all the ministers in his office." Then he asked, "Before you go in, can I have a private word with you, Floyd?"

"Of course," Floyd agreed. He didn't need his discernment because his innermost being *felt* the newness of Benny. However, his discernment did tell him what it was about. He turned to the others and instructed, "Y'all go on ahead. I'll join you in just a few."

†††

The group from the estate had parked and

were unloading their vehicles. When Ditto saw Smittie leave Floyd alone with Benny. He inquired, "I wonder what that's about?"

Leroy still didn't like the man. "Too bad I am no longer on the force. Otherwise I would arrest him for disturbing the peace."

Matthew looked towards the church and huffed. He was not in the mood for Benny to give his father anymore grief. Not on a day like today. "I don't know, but I am going to find out," he replied, and angrily stalked towards them. Ditto, Leroy, and JR struck out behind him.

Mark noticed them when he closed the hatch on his SUV. He shouted across the lot, "What's going on?" His discernment kicked in when he saw *who* they were making their way towards. He shouted, "Wait! It's not what you guys think!" Then he and all of his male cousins got in behind them.

Mark's shout caught Floyd and Benny's attention. When Benny saw Floyd's sons and nephews moving towards them, he didn't think anything of it. He assumed they were going to go through the garage, to unlock the door by the stairs that led to the kitchen. He suggested, "Let's walk around the corner of the building and talk."

Floyd recognized the expressions on his son and nephews' faces. "Hold on a minute," he insisted, and stepped in front of Benny.

†††

"Are you giving my father a hard time again,

Benny?" Matthew barked even before he reached them.

"What's your gripe with my uncle now, Benny?" Leroy questioned.

"Don't you ever get tired of being a thorn in my uncle's side?" Ditto asked.

Benny went to explain himself, but Floyd stopped him. "Since when do you step up to an *elder* like that, Matthew? Brotha Benny is old enough to be all three of you all's father. You either address him as Brotha Benny, or Mr. Benny. And don't ever let me hear y'all speak to him in that disrespectful tone again. Y'all understand me?" he sharply reprimanded.

"What's the big deal? We call Jared, Ev, and Smooth by their names," Leroy challenged.

The Walker brothers walked up in time to hear the conversation. E hit Leroy on the back of his head. "You do like you are told, boy. Brotha Benny is *my* age. Y'all ain't got no business calling him by his name."

Howard glared at Ditto. "Especially with an attitude. Your mother and I didn't raise you like *that,* Howard."

"What is this about, Floyd?" H asked.

"Benny and I were about to discuss my re-ordaining him today. These boys got all bent out of shape when they saw us talking."

Benny raised his brows. "You already *knew* what I wanted, Floyd?"

Floyd nodded. "Of course I did, and it will be

my *pleasure*."

"Thank you. That means a great deal to me. Do you think Alden will be offended? The last thing I want is to cause trouble between the two of you."

"Let me worry about that."

"Alright," Benny replied. Then he looked at Matthew, Leroy, and Ditto, and back at Floyd. "Don't be too hard on them for coming to your defense. Especially after the way I've treated you in the past."

"Let's suppose, for argument's sake, that it had been what you boys thought. Since when has Floyd needed any one of you to fight *his* battle?" Clyde questioned.

"Verbally or otherwise," Luther injected.

"Never," H forcefully declared. Then he reprimanded, "E is right. Benny is our age. None of you had any business going at an elder, regardless of what you *thought* was happening. Furthermore, you boys know where your zip code *ends*, and my brothers and mine's *begins*. You all better not ever cross that cemented line again."

Mark had been quiet the entire time because he felt bad for his brother and cousins. Mostly because he'd never shared with them what happened at the church every day. Mainly, he really felt bad for Brotha Benny over the way they'd attacked him. He understood their reasoning, seeing that the last time they saw Benny, he was going off on his father. But their aggressive attack had no legs this time. He finally spoke up, "He is not the same Brotha Benny we all once knew. This Brotha Benny has been driving the church bus, picking up people who don't have cars. Not just on Sundays, but also during the week. He's at the church Monday through Friday, from open to close, helping wherever he is needed. He even brings us lunch *every day*."

"What?" Floyd asked.

"He said it's the least he can do, since you are making us work for free, Uncle Floyd," Aden falsely reported.

"I did *not* say that, Aden," Benny denied and laughed. "I bring lunch for the seniors who come to the church every day. *And* the church reimburses me from the welfare offering. The staff gets the *leftovers*."

Floyd chuckled and patted his arm. "Come on, let's go in, Benny."

"Not until these boys apologize," Clyde demanded.

"Be quick about it too," Luther insisted and popped JR on the back of his head.

"Why you hit me? I didn't say anything."

"You wanted to. You just didn't get it out before Floyd spoke up," Luther accused.

The Walker brothers roared when all of their *grown* sons moved away from them, to keep from getting hit. Then they shamefully, but sincerely apologized.

Benny graciously accepted their apology, "Trust me, I understand." Then he informed Mark, Aden, Candace, and Betty Jean, "Alden wants all the ministers to join him in his office, for a moment of prayer, before we greet our guests at the doors."

Then he, Floyd, and the ministers walked in the garage, and let the door down. Everybody else walked back across the parking lot to finish unloading the cars.

CHAPTER 22

The choir was singing 'Oh Come All Ye Faithful' when the ministers and Deacons entered the sanctuary. Alden and Capri, and their spouses, sat on the front row of the center pews. Benny escorted the guest ministers to the pulpit. Then he placed Floyd's Bible on the dais. Floyd shook his hand, and said, "Thank you."

Benny gripped his hand and forearm. "Any time, *Good Reverend.*" Then he made his way to the front row.

Some in the congregation's eyes rolled from side to side, as they whispered to each other; while slightly jerking their heads towards them. Floyd noticed the *messy* expressions on their faces. He chuckled, but not in a comical manner. When the choir finished singing, he said, "There is no greater miracle than a *changed* heart. Didn't the most prolific New Testament *murderer* of Christians, Paul, say 'But this one thing *I* do?' There were some who continuously reminded him of his past." He looked down at the front row and said, "But Paul said, *"I press on'*, Brother Benny."

Benny waved an affirming hand in the air. Floyd turned his eyes back to the members and asked, "Didn't a change come over you when Jesus came into your *hearts?* I know it did for me and your pastor."

You'd better know it, Floyd," Alden bore witness.

That sparked the organist to tune up the keyboard. Freeney and the choir joined in softly singing, "Something happened! That made a *change* in me! Woo, woo!"

Floyd noticed that the aisles were lined with several dozen of *his* old gang members. They were dressed in black walking suits, with quarter length sleeves. Each one wore a black beret with gold front facing embossed lettering that said, "Usher." They were all facing him. When they saw him looking at them, they placed their right hands over their hearts. He placed his hand over his heart, and passionately crooned, "Jesus stepped in."

The choir rang out, "And made a change in me!" and the entire church went up!!

†††

When everybody settled down, he said, "I came today to install your pastor and your assistant pastor. However, it would be remiss of me not to say anything about the birth of Christ, seeing that it is the *designated* day we celebrate His birth. Nevertheless, I won't be long."

Someone teased, "Yeah right, Pastor Floyd,"

and the church went up in laughter.

Floyd didn't open his Bible, and he didn't give a text. He just chuckled and begged, "Indulge me for just a moment, while I tell you a story."

"Alright Preacha!"

"There was a city, on the northern tip of the promised land, called *Galilee*. Within this city, in the upper mountainous region, there was a small nomad town called *Nazareth*. The residents of Nazareth were so poor they slept under the same roof as their sheep and oxen. When the weather permitted it, they slept *on* the roof, while their beasts slept *under* it. Residing in this town was a young peasant girl, name *Mary*. Although engaged to be married, to a carpenter name *Joseph*, Mary was still a *virgin*. Which by the way was more uncommon in those days than it is now. See, women in those days were treated as *the spoils* of war. Men were allowed to do what they wanted to whomever they wanted. That in itself speaks volumes to Joseph's character, but that's another sermon."

"Take your time, Preacher!"

"One day the Angel of the Lord, Gabriel came to Mary with a message, 'Hail, thou art *highly* favored'. Mary was unnerved because she didn't know who this stranger was, what he wanted, or what he meant. Was he a marauder, who planned on stealing the meager belongings her family had? Gabriel sensed her nervousness and said, 'Do not be afraid. You have found favor with *God*'. Then he went on to prophesy, 'You will conceive and give birth to a son, and you are to call him Jesus'. Mary said, 'How can that be, I ain't even slept with the man I've pledged to marry, let alone any other man'. Gabriel informed her that He will be the son of the Most High God'."

He paused and chuckled. "I can hear this scenario playing out in current day, with you women responding in a variety of slang, "You trippin, negro!' 'If you don't step off!' 'Get the *bleep* out of Dodge'! 'The Devil *is* a lie!'"

The church went up in roaring laughter. Gabriel was sitting in the congregation, with his brothers. They *all* howled in Floyd's *ear.* Floyd chuckled and continued, "Gabriel went on to tell Mary that her son would be seated on the throne of His father, David, and that He would reign over Jacob's descendants *forever.* Still not convinced she once again questioned how, seeing that she was a virgin. Gabriel informed her the Most High would send His spirit to overshadow her and plant His seed in her womb. She was like, 'Alright. If it be God's will.'"

He paused and said, "Some of y'all would've been thinking, 'If this ain't no joke, how in the world am I going to explain *this.* Ain't no way I can trick him into believing he's the *baby daddy!*'"

Remembering what state they were in, Capri squealed so loud, that everybody in the sanctuary jumped. Then she squeaked, "Hoosier daddy!" The congregation broke out in roaring laughter again.

H looked at E and declared, "That boy is a

stone *fool!"*

E was laughing too hard to respond outloud. He replied with his mind, *"Capri is too! Can you see those two co-pastoring?"*

"Once Mary confirmed that she *was* pregnant, she broke down and told her, soon to be executioner, boyfriend. That brotha was all you can eat, chili pepper hot. And he did not believe her story for a minute."

He perused the congregation at the men. "None of y'all would believe it either. I can hear y'all now, 'How you gon' play me! You must think I'm a fool! While you put me on lockdown, you been lettin' some other brotha hit that! Ain't that a *itch!* Give me my *bleep* ring back and lose my *bleeper bleeping* number!!"

Every man in the sanctuary, including those behind him, in the pulpit and choir, came to their feet. All of them voicetriously agreeing, "Sho you right, Pastor," one shouted.

"You got that right, preacher," one of the men shouted from the back.

"If she knows what's good for her, she'd call me on the *phone*, from a *hidden* location, with that message. Otherwise I'm putting a *serious tappin'* on that girl," one shamelessly threatened.

All the men turned and stared at him. Alden frowned when he saw it was the same boy he'd run out of his office. The Watchers audibly growled. Floyd furrowed his brows. Tapping had dual meanings in today's society. Did he mean he'd *rape* or *beat* her? Both were *unacceptable*. He spoke directly to the young man, "Thankfully, *Joseph* was a *God-fearing* man, son. He decided to put her away, so the men in their town wouldn't *kill* her. As was the custom for loose women, in those days."

Then he turned his attention to the women and said, "Ain't y'all sistahs glad that's no longer the *law* of the land? Or that, *that* young man is not *your* man?"

The young man bowed his head when every woman in the sanctuary thunderously clapped and shouted, "Amen, Pastor Floyd."

Lillian shouted, "If he were mine, he would be the one that got tapped."

"Say that, cuz," Dawn co-signed.

"Gabriel appeared to Joseph in a dream and confirmed everything that Mary told him. I often wondered why he came to Mary while she was *awake,* but to Joseph while he was *asleep.* I've come to believe it was because Joseph wouldn't listen to Mary, so you know he wasn't going to listen to no brotha. Seeing that Archangels have the same physical attributes as we have, he might've even accused Gabriel, 'That's *yo* baby!'"

The members laughed again and so did the Watchers. The homeless and the wounded soldiers were in stitches. Many of them had never heard a preacher preach like this. They thought to themselves that if they had, their lives might've turned out differently. Gabriel's brothers looked at him and roared outloud.

"Anyway, Joseph believed what he heard in his dream. He readily married her, but they did not consummate their marriage until after she had the baby."

"Amen."

"Then came the newly dreaded *then*, and the dreaded *now*, tax season. It was decreed that every man had to go back to the city of their lineage to pay. So, Joseph, also being from the house of David, prepared for the seventy-mile journey south to *Judea*, which is a suburb of *Bethlehem*. As was customary, he packed their *linen cloths*. That was so that in the event they died on the road, they could be *swaddled* in it, and properly buried. While traversing Mary goes into *labor*. Thankfully, they'd reached their destination, but there were no vacancies in any of the inns. One inn keeper realizing Mary was in labor, offers them the stable. It was no biggy for them, because remember they lived in Nazareth, and slept under the same roof as their animals *anyway*. Therefore, even if they hadn't been on the road she would've still given birth with the oxen and other beasts watching."

"Go on and tell the story, Floyd," Jared encouraged from behind him.

"Mary finally gives birth to Jesus. He's bloody, cold, naked, shivering and crying. She takes out *her* death cloth and swaddles *Him* in it." He paused and looked behind him. Then he pointed at Mark and reported, "My son and my nephew, Henry, said Jesus was *wrapped in death*, the moment he took his first breath."

"Yes! Yes!" Mark and Henry validated.

"Eight days after His birth they made their way to the temple. That was so that Jesus could be circumcised, in keeping with the *Abrahamic* covenant. Gabriel appeared to Joseph in another dream that night. This time he tells him not to go back home, because King Herod has sent out a decree to kill all baby boys. He instructs him to take his family down to Egypt. Joseph questions that because he knew that God had said for no Hebrew to ever go back to Egypt. In fact, He said that He would kill anybody who did. *I* believe they misunderstood what God was saying."

"Break it down, Floyd," Benny shouted.

"God's instructions were for them to not go to Egypt to *purchase* or *trade* anything. Specifically, the horse and chariots that the Egyptians had. *I* believe that could've been because that was how they got trapped in Egypt in the first place. If you recall, Jacob sent his sons there with gold to trade for grain. And it took four hundred years for them to be delivered."

"True that," Tommie agreed.

"I am sure that Gabriel assured them that even the Romans knew that they weren't allow to go to Egypt. That meant that Herod's men wouldn't bother to look for them there."

Gabriel verbally co-signed, "Amen."

"So Joseph packs up his family and they go to Egypt. They stay until King Herod dies, around

4AD. Then they make their way back home to Nazareth, where Jesus lived throughout His childhood and young adult years. The Bible doesn't record anything about His childhood, except *briefly* at the age of *thirteen*. When He finally steps out, He does so at age *thirty*. That is when He leaves the mountainous region, and walks the same path as a *man*, that He took as an unborn baby in *Mary's womb*. The same seventy miles, from Nazareth to Judea. Cause, five miles away was where He was *predestined* to be crucified, on Calvary's mountain. So that He could, over two thousand years later, extend *grace* to an old *gangbanging* sinner like *me*."

Sal stood up and shouted, "Floyd!"

Stones stood up all over the sanctuary and shouted, "Floyd! Floyd! Floyd!"

He clapped his hands and shouted, "They swaddled my *Lord* in linen, on the day He was born. They swaddled my *Savior* in linen, on the day He died!"

His brothers came to their feet shouting, "Preach! Preach, Sonny man! Preach, boy!"

He reared back and hooped, "You can't tell the story of Jesus, without telling it from the *cradle* to the *grave!*"

All over the church the people egged him on. He propped his hands on his hips and hooped, "You gotta tell it from the *borrowed* womb to the *borrowed* tomb."

Benny stood up clapping and shouting, "Preach, Good Reverend! Preach! Preach!"

"Our Lord and Savior inhaled His *first* breath and expelled His *last* breath, on the *same* ground, Benny!" With handkerchief in hand, he grabbed his ear, swirled around towards the ministers, and hooped, "On the *same* cursed ground where Cain's blood *cried out*."

The ministers jumped to their feet. "Say it! Say it! Tell it! We with you!"

"My Lord was born and died, on the *same* ground where *Adam* sinned, and *all* was *lost*. On that *holy ground*, once called *Eden!* On that same ground, He restored our lost souls! And brought us back in fellowship with God!"

"Come on, Preacher!"

"Isaiah prophesied that He shall be called Immanuel! Meaning, '*God with us!*' I found out for myself, a *loooong* time ago, that He's a *wonderful* counselor, a *mighty* God, *everlasting* Father, and *Prince* of peace!" He *abruptly* stopped, wiped his mouth, turned back toward the congregation, and said, "I'll leave it there."

"Preach on, Pastor," Frank insisted.

"Don't stop, Reverend," Lula begged.

Pleas went on and on. Floyd moaned, "Jesus," and then crooned, "What a *wonderful* child." He abruptly stopped again and fanned his hands from side to side. "I have to be *obedient* to Holy," he explained. Then he looked behind him at the ministers, and instructed, "Join me at the altar."

CHAPTER 23

When Floyd and the ministers reached the altar he stood in front of the communion table, with them on each side of him. That table was in front of the center pews, where Alden, Capri, their families, and the Archangels were seated. He extended his hands and beckoned Alden and Antionette to join him.

Once they made their way to the altar he said to the congregation, "I told you all of this because your new pastor, Alden, was *born* in Gary, Indiana. Five miles from Grace. Like Jesus, his parents moved him across the country when he was *three years old.* He grew up poor, in the ghetto of Compton, California. Like me, he was a gangbanger for a while. But Jesus didn't call the self-righteous religious folks to be His disciples. He said, 'I didn't come to call the *righteous,* but the *sinners* into repentance.' The gangbangers, gamblers, mobsters, drug dealers, tax collectors, harlots, and thieves."

"Go on and preach anyhow, Floyd," Sal encouraged.

"Like Jesus's ministry, Alden's ministry

didn't start out in a building, preaching to well-dressed church folk. He preached on the ghetto streets, to lost, disillusioned, and downtrodden sinners. When God was ready, He called His servant *back home*, and offered him *Grace*. This *glass* building is where this once gangbanger *had* to be. His past lets the lost know that if God can change and accept him, He can change and accept them."

Alden had not put that together. Now he knew why Floyd had designed this building. His eyes were watery when he mumbled, "Yes sah! Grace is sufficient!"

Floyd turned toward Alden. "God told Moses to consecrate Aaron at the door of the temple, in *front* of the Israelites. That was so that they would know that Aaron was *His* chosen High Priest, above all of the Levites. I am sorry that it has taken me three years to consecrate you, Alden. God knows it wasn't intentional."

"I understand how it happened, Floyd," Alden assured him.

"Jesus is the High Priest now, therefore there is no need for consecration at the door of the temple. Nevertheless, there is still a need for *anointing* of any pastor that *God* has chosen, as all of the priests had to be anointed," Floyd explained.

Then he directed Jared to grab the bottle of blessed oil off the communion table. Jared did and opened it. Floyd opened his left hand and Jared poured some of the oil in his palm. Floyd dipped the ring finger of his right hand in the oil. Then he sprinkled it on Alden's *right* ear and rubbed it on the *thumb* of his right hand, while explaining, "Listen with a *right* and *holy* ear to the needs of your congregation, as well as for the direction of Holy. No matter what, use your hands in *righteous* service and praise for God." He squatted down and removed Alden's right shoe and sock. Then he anointed his big toe, while declaring *and* instructing, "Grace may be *my* bitter cup, but it is *your* cross to bear. Walk confidently, but circumspect, while carrying it. If you do these five things, your cup will run over with goodness and mercy, all the days of your life, Alden." He stood up and placed his oil filled palm on Alden's head, said, "Thou anointed my head with oil," and fervently prayed over him.

Alden and Antionette were both a teary mess. He wiped his eyes and said, "Thank you, Floyd."

Floyd hugged him and then beckoned Capri and Sterling to join them. When they walked up, he said, "Mary of Magdala was Jesus's most faithful disciple. While the men ran for cover, she was with him right up to the end. Alden picked you to be his *assistant* pastor, not an *associate* pastor. It is your responsibility to help him carry his cross. And make no mistake about it, pastorship *is* a cross. Jesus said, 'If anyone would come after me, they must deny themself, take up their *cross* and follow me.' Alden's cross will sometimes get too *heavy*, Capri. Every now and again, he *will* become tired and weak, and will stumble from the weight. Don't *you* be dismayed or lose heart. Just step up and help him *carry it*, daughter. Always remember that Simon of Cyrene helped Jesus carry that old *rugged* cross, when *He* stumbled from the weight of it."

Capri's entire family and all of her friends from Texas and North Carolina, were sitting behind them, in the center row. Her mother and mother-in-law, Cordia and Freda were openly weeping. So were her cousins Brandi, Wanda, and their mother, Claudia. Her sister, Mercedes was whimpering on her husband, Jacque's chest. Her brother, father, father-in-law, and uncle, Monty, Edwin, Tavis, and Marshall, were silently wiping their eyes. As were the 'Sanctioned' mates. The Archangels were singing shouts of joy, in her mind.

Tears were streaming down her face when she sobbed, "Yes, sir."

Floyd opened his palm to Jared. Jared once again poured the oil in it. Then he anointed her in the same manner in which he anointed Alden and prayed over her.

He wiped his hands on the pre-moistened towel Tommie handed him. Then he addressed Antionette and Sterling, "Your roles are to daily cover your spouses in prayer, be supportive of them, and their ministry. Make sure their homes are peaceful and loving."

"Yes, sir."

He kissed Antionette's right cheek and shook Sterling's hand, and instructed, "The two of you can be seated."

Then he embraced Alden's forearm and

whispered in his ear, "It's getting close to lunchtime. I'm sure the guests are getting hungry. Would you allow me the honor of ordaining and installing your Deacons, and Deaconesses?"

Alden had never installed or ordained anyone before. He wasn't even sure he knew the difference. He'd been up all-night googling instructions on how to do it. He'd even checked YouTube. Some of the videos of actual services were *disgusting*. Never once did he think about opening the Bible and going to *Leviticus* for instructions, like Floyd evidently had done. Or maybe his pastor just remembered those ceremonial scriptures. He was sure that every pastor under Floyd's leadership could learn a thing or two from him. "By all means, Floyd."

†††

Floyd turned his attention to the front row of the right-side pews. Frank, Benny, Bill, and Dedrick were sitting closest to the center aisle. He wasn't surprised to see Jorge and Carlos, Justin's brothers, sitting with them. Alden had already informed him of those he'd selected. Although Frank was already an ordained Deacon, he was sitting with them because he was Alden's *head* deacon. Benny had also been ordained but wanted a do-over. He hadn't understood that at first, but he did now. Bill and Dedrick were the ex-gangbangers, now junior Deacons. He extended his hand and said, "Join us on the altar."

Once they made their way to the altar, Floyd

walked over and stood in front of Benny. "I didn't understand why you needed to be ordained again, since I'd already ordained you. But I get it now. It's about a new heart for you."

"And a right spirit," Benny explained.

"*1st Timothy* says that a Deacon must be worthy of respect and *sincere,*" Floyd quoted and patted his arm. Then he moved on down the line, while he continued to quote Timothy, with a twist, "It does not say that you can't have a glass of wine or two. It says not given to *much* wine. Which means not an alcoholic. That is because as leaders of the church, you must be in control of your *body* and *mind.* You must be able to teach God's word, in the event your pastor or assistant pastor is unavailable. You must be able to manage your *own* homes. If you can't, how can you manage *God's* house." He went on and on with what is expected of Deacons. He finally ended with his own input, "A Deacon must be an unwavering *tither.* That's because you don't *give* tithes, you *pay* them. If you don't, God says that you are robbing Him. I don't know about Alden, but I have never let a thief hold even the smallest office in my church."

"Amen, Floyd," Alden agreed.

"From what I know of you men, Alden has chosen a strong group of men. Ones who hold the sanctity of family as a must. That's good."

Then he picked up the bottle of blessed oil, poured some in Capri, Sal, Betty, Candace, Mark, and Aden's palms, and told them what to do. As they stood in front of each of the newly installed Deacons, they anointed their heads with the oil. Floyd, and all the ministers who were senior *pastors* of their own congregation, Alden, Jared, and Tommie came right behind them and prayed over each one.

When they finished praying, Floyd shook their hands. Then he instructed them to stand on both sides of the ministers.

†††

His gaze fell on the Deaconesses. The church accountant, Margaret Scott was sitting further down the row, along with six women: Ernest's wife, *Lisa Downey,* Darious's wife, *Sherell Burns-Moulden*, Blake's wife, *Myra O'Malley*, John's wife, *Suzette Lofton,* Marius's wife, *Elaine Phillips*, *and* Steady Groove's wife, *Gladys Walton.* He instructed them to join him at the altar.

Once they were standing in front of him, he said, "In the 6th chapter of Acts, the disciples and apostles were griping because they didn't feel that they should ignore Jesus's instruction to carry the word, in order to take care of the needy. Everyone agreed that it was a valid complaint. The solution to this problem was given in the 3rd verse. 'Wherefore, brethren, look ye out amongst you seven men of honest report, full of the Holy Ghost and wisdom, whom we may appoint over *this* business.' Many are confused about this passage. They have been taught that the seven, quote unquote, are the *Deacons*, but that is a *misinterpretation.* You understand that when they refer to waiting on tables," he said and chuckled. "Keep in mind that they chose *men* because in those days women had no rights, or leadership roles, in any aspect of their lives. Other than preparing the meals. That mindset is different in today's churches *and* homes. In fact, I've never known a man who is able to handle his household finances as well as his wife. I know my wife, MeiLi can stretch a dollar far beyond *my* ability."

Men all over the church stood up and clapped their agreement. "Amen, Pastor," Frank Leavy co-signed.

"In Proverbs 1:20-33, wisdom is personified as *female.* In saying that, Pastor Gaines has chosen wisely when he chose *all* women to handle Grace's finances," Floyd complimented. Then he went down the line anointing all of their heads with oil. Alden, Capri, Jared, Tommie, Sal, Aden, and Mark immediately embraced the crowns of their heads and prayed over them.

When the ceremony was complete, Floyd looked out at the congregation and said, "Let the church say *amen*, to your new Pastor, Assistant Pastor, Deacons and Deaconesses."

"Amen."

†††

Seeing that he was Alden's pastor, Floyd realized that there was one more step that needed to be taken. He extended the righthand of fellowship to both, Alden, and Capri. "Now you are both officially members of Grace." Then he said, "Come on, Grace, welcome your pastor and assistant pastor."

The congregation stood up. Then in an orderly manner directed by the ushers, from the last pews to the front ones, they marched down the aisle. The choir joyously started to sing, 'What a Fellowship', as the members shook their hands and hugged them.

Alden's children and grandchildren came up to him together. They were all members but only *bench members*. His son, Alden Jr. spoke for his four siblings, "We could not be prouder of you, Dad. Whatever you want us to do just say the word. You and your ministry have all of our support."

His children Were amazing singers, and musicians. Piano, organ, drums, and guitar. They all just had a *natural* gift. He hugged every one of them and said, "You all know what I want, son."

Cordia hugged Capricious and rocked her back and forward. "I am so proud of you, Capri. From the time you were a teenager, you never put God in a box. You were right. There ain't a box big enough, baby."

Her sons and daughters encircled her and kissed and kissed and kissed and kissed her. "We love you, Mama," Sterling Jr. declared.

Her father, Edwin hugged her and teasingly whispered, "I see you are still hanging around with gangbangers."

She burst out laughing. "I guess I am, but Alden and Floyd are gangbangers for God."

He pulled away and caressed her cheek. She looked so much like his mother it was amazing. "I have always been proud of you, Capri. Always," he declared and kissed her cheek.

Chamuel kissed her soaked cheek. "I told you that God had plans for you. Did I not?"

Sterling wiped his wife's cheek. "Show them what you got, girl!" She laughed and hugged him.

After the fellowship, Floyd and the other ministers went back to the pulpit. Alden and Capri stood on the altar, along with the Deacons and Deaconesses. Then Alden opened the doors of the church, while the choir sang, "Come Unto Jesus, While You Have Time."

Many of the homeless and soldiers made their way to the altar. Martha Ruff was so grateful to finally have a warm place to sleep. She knew that God had put it on those men's hearts to help her. When the choir sang, "He will make your life brand new," she went down at Capri's feet moaning, "Thank you, Jesus!"

The ushers went to help her up, but Capri stopped them. Then she knelt down on her knees, in front of her. With tears running down her own face, she hugged her and encouraged, "He'll take care of you, sistah." Then they both started shouting. The two of them had people crying all over the sanctuary.

CHRISTMAS

DINNER

AND

FELLOWSHIP

12:00 - NOON

CHAPTER 24

Many of the guests weren't aware that Grace was serving dinner, even though they smelled the aroma permeating the sanctuary. Most of the members had no plans on staying because they cooked at home for their families, and out of town guests. Plus, their children were itching to get home to their gifts.

As always, Pastor Alden made the usual announcement, prior to the benediction, "We serve dinner every year after Christmas service. We don't allow carry-outs, because we want our guests, and members, to stay and *fellowship* with us. This year we've done something a little different. Instead of ordering food from a restaurant chain, we've utilized some of our own." Then he pointed in the pulpit and added, "Youth Pastor, Aden Walker's wife, Dee, and her group of chefs, have prepared a feast, in the dining hall. Let me tell y'all something. Y'all ain't even tasted homecooked food until you've tasted hers. That young lady will have all of you committing the sin of *gluttony*. Begging for more, even though there's no room in the inn."

Everybody from the estate proudly co-signed, "Amen!"

Alden looked up in the pulpit at Floyd and winked. Then he turned back around and announced, "Which reminds me, Galilee will not be open this coming week."

Floyd could see some of them sitting in Galilee confessing, *"I pigged out, Pastor. Pray for me."* He kept a straight face but, he and the other ministers howled in each other's ears.

"That melanin deficient sistah's cooking will make every woman in this church want to sit under her tutelage," Antionette boasted.

No one in the congregation was offended by the way that she'd described Dee. That's because they were a melting pot of all races. And, like most Americans, every race came in a scale of skin tones: Black, dark brown, light brown, tan, and White.

Under Floyd's leadership, they'd learned to be proud of their heritage, and to celebrate each other's. He'd explained that once they accepted Christ, the color of their skin no longer defined or separated their race *or* heritage. He said Christian was now their race, and joint heir with Christ their heritage. Of course that was after he put some people out of Grace because of their disdain for his Chinese wife, MeiLi. He told them that there was no room for *racism* at Grace Tabernacle. He didn't care what skin tone the racist was.

Alden chuckled at his wife's comment, but validated her, "We kid you not! Those of you who can stay, are in for a *treat*."

"We only ask that the members allow the welcoming committee to escort our invited local guests to the hall first," Capri directed. She added 'local' so the members would not think that she meant her and Alden's out of town family members. Both of them had already informed their families that the homeless and soldiers would be seated first.

"Will everybody please stand," Alden instructed. They all rose to their feet, and he said the benediction. Then they sat back down as he and the ministers, deacons, deaconesses, and their spouses, promptly made their way to the various doors. The congregation noticed, for the first time, that they'd dressed *uniformly*. They were all dressed in white collarless suits, blue shirts, and blouses. The men wore white and blue striped neck ties. The women had white and blue striped scarfs draped over their right shoulders.

When they made it to their pre-appointed door, Alden instructed, "All who arrived on buses, please make your way to the door closest to you."

Once those standing at the various doors had their guests lined up in the hallway, they informed them, "Once we get to the dining hall, feel free to sit at any table you want."

Then they themselves *paused* when they got to the door of the hall. That's because the decorations were in no way what any of them had envisioned. It was much, *much,* more than they imagined.

†††

The walls along the chair rails were garnished with drooping blue garland, entwined with tiny Christmas lights. Above the garland, a mural of the Nativity scene had been painted on large billboards and fastened to one entire wall. Directly across from it, on the facing wall, was a mural of the crucifixion, also fastened to the wall. Alden spoke to Floyd's mind, *"Did you tell them what your sermon was going to be about."*

Floyd smiled one-sided. *"No. Those that live on the estate have always known that you can't imagine the birth of Christ, without imagining His death."*

Alden nodded and casted his eyes back at the decorations. There were one hundred and twenty cherrywood tables, with bear-claw legs, draped with white linen tablecloths. Six crystal vases served as the center pieces for each table. Each one filled with silver pinecones and blue ornaments. Silver silk tinsel garland snaked by white snowflakes, ran the length of the tables. Twelve silver plate chargers were in place, on each table, with neatly folded blue linen napkins resting on them. A holiday gift card was tucked within the folds of the napkins.

Diamond cut crystal glasses were placed next to the chargers, at the eleven o'clock position. Frosted crystal cups, on matching saucers, sat to the right of each charger. Sterling silverware was positioned on each side of the chargers. Forks to the left. Knives and spoons to the right. The *armed* cherrywood chairs were all heavily cushioned on the back and seat, with white silk.

Floyd spoke to his daughter's and her crew's minds, *"You young ladies really outdid yourselves!"*

Symphony smiled at her father's remark, and explained, *"We didn't want this dinner to resemble a soup kitchen."*

"Nor did we want our guests to feel like this was a handout," Lillian added.

"So, we pulled out all the stops to make the homeless, the soldiers, and the lonely feel their worth," Cinquetta explained.

"Brock stepped up and provided what our committee could not. Like this many cherrywood tables and chairs," Faith reported.

"I provided what you asked for, but you ladies put this together. It is stunning, y'all," Brock complimented. Then he added, *"H and Ditto. Your crews have added a touch of sho-nuff class."*

†††

H and Ditto's crew fell way short of one hundred. They'd had to enlist many of the field Watchers and Alter Egos to assist them. They were standing at each table, with their left arms behind them, dressed in white tuxedos, blue shirts, and white ties. An Ultimate Watcher, his second, and a host of Archangels, dressed in everyday clothing, were standing at the heads of each table. Some were in jeans and sweatshirts, others in dress pants and sweaters. Their attire was to make those they'd be sitting with feel comfortable. Those who had their mates, their mates were standing at the foot of the table, dressed in a like manner.

Per Jodi's instructions, her cousin, Anita and Jeremiel were seated at the table to her and Brock's left. She hugged Anita and said, "It's been a minute, girlfriend."

"More than, but it's good to see you, cuz," Anita greeted. Then she looked over Jodi's shoulder and said, "Look who I brought with me."

Jodi turned around, smiled, and gleefully expressed, "Ticola! I didn't know you were coming."

"Girl, please. I wasn't about to miss Capri's installation. Seeing you again is the icing on the cake."

"Why didn't you tell me?"

"I wanted to surprise you."

They talked often but hadn't seen one another in a few years. They were more than excited to see each other. They hugged and rocked each other back and forth, for a minute or two. Jodi finally pulled away and insisted, "You and Zerachiel sit at this table on our right."

"Our mates already pre-arranged that, girl. Zerachiel knew I was going to give him the *business* if he didn't. We're staying in town until New Year's Eve."

"On the estate?"

"Where else?"

✝✝✝

Brock spoke to Ariel's mind, *"Please don't ruin this dinner for these people!"*

Ariel grinned and promised, *"I'll behave, just for you. Merry Christmas, nephew."* His brothers and Brock roared.

Ditto spoke to his and H's crews' minds, *"Smile everybody. This is it."*

"Also remember to pull the chairs out for the women," H instructed.

"We got this, Grandpa," Addison spoke for the crews.

"It's a lot more than we expected. It's a good thing we ate while service was going on," Henry mused. All of the workers had eaten at eleven, so they'd be able to work without being hungry.

"I just said the same thing, Henry," Shona voiced. She was on the dessert team.

✝✝✝

None of their guests could believe how formal everything was. They were all expecting the usual folding tables, with plastic tablecloths, paper plates and cups. Some had never sat at a table this elegant, even before they became homeless. And those men dressed in the white tuxes blew them away. They silently moved forward, left, and right, and took the first *available* seat. Once the guests were seated, the members filed in and took whatever seats were left. They were as surprised over the setting, as their guests had been. Lula made her way to the table where Akibeel was standing. She hugged him and kissed his cheek. Then she spoke to his mind, *"I was afraid I wouldn't get a seat with you, son."*

He hugged her tight and confessed, *"I made sure no one wanted this one next to me."*

She laughed, sat down, and then asked, *"Where are Maria and Mateo?"*

"Maria is working with the group that will fill the glasses, and coffee cups. Mateo is at the children's tables."

They both smiled when Mateo ran over and hugged her. "Hi, Grandma Lula."

She hugged him and kissed his cheek. "Hey, Baby. You look so handsome."

He pulled away, said, "I gotta go! Bye!" and ran back to the children's table.

That did Lula's heart all the good in the world.

†††

To Alden's delight, quite a few of the members stayed who'd never stayed before. Many of them were struggling to make ends meet. The committees had originally said fifty tables for the adults, and twenty for the children. They had placed one hundred and twenty instead. He was grateful for their forethought because there were only two empty tables. But those two were for the ministers, deacons, deaconesses, their spouses, and Michael and Verenda.

He shook a few of his members' hands as

they entered, and said, "I'm glad that you all decided to join us."

"After your rave review, we had to check this woman's food out," most of them admitted.

He laughed because he knew they'd be grateful that they stayed, and for more than one reason. "Trust me. You are all in for a *bountiful* blessing."

Sal had already been assigned to say grace. Once everyone was seated, he stood in the middle of the floor and prayed, "We thank you, Father, for this body of willing servants. The cooks, decorators, greeters, servers, water carriers, dishwashers, and trash collectors. Thank you *mostly* for those who you have sent to fellowship and sup with us. We thank you for Pastor Alden, and Grace's willingness to allow us to partner with them in hosting this meal. We ask that you bless them in a mighty way. Press it down, shake it together, until they have no room to receive it. We ask this, in the powerful name of Jesus. Amen."

"So be it," Smooth translated.

Everyone in the hall echoed, "So be it."

CHAPTER 25

The minute Sal finished praying, Aden and Mark walked to the center of the floor. "Everyone please stay in your seats. The waiters will bring your meal to you," Aden instructed.

The disruptive young man that Alden complained about, was sitting at Brock's table, next to him. Everyone knew Brock had tinkered with his mind and compelled him to do so. He shouted, "What y'all serving, anyway? I hope it ain't no stinkin' chitlins!"

"And so what if it is?" Brock sternly questioned. "Do you know how rude it is for you to demand what someone should or should not serve. Especially when it is free?"

"I don't like chitlins," the young man mumbled.

"What is your name, son?"

"Jaheem."

Brock squinted and then shook his head because his behavior certainly didn't live up to his name. He searched the boy's memories and sighed. Now he understood. He was one of Deuce's friend,

Dr. Norris's eleven siblings. He was only sixteen and acted out because he couldn't get any attention at home. Not with so many brothers and sisters. His father was an over-the-road truckdriver, who was gone for weeks at a time. His mother did what she could, but there wasn't enough of her to go around. His behavior drove home what Jodi had said all along, *'You shouldn't have more children than you can emotionally support.'* Then he recalled *why* Joseph's brothers had sold him.

He shook his head again and continued to reprimand the boy, "Even so, Jaheem, there is no reason for you to behave in this manner. If by chance they do serve chitlins, there will be other dishes on your plate. Just eat what you like and leave what you don't."

"My mother makes us eat everything on our plate. Even chitlins," he griped.

"This ain't your mother's table, son."

Jaheem smiled for the first time. Mainly because an adult was showing him some much needed attention. "Okay. What is *your* name?*"

"My name is Brock. Now would you like to go sit with the other teenagers?"

Jaheem looked across the room and saw all the children. It looked like his kitchen table at home. He shook his head. "Can I stay here with you, Mr. Brock?"

Brock smiled, nodded, and stipulated, "Only if you *behave*. And promise me that you will stop antagonizing Pastor Gaines."

Jaheem smiled sheepishly. "Okay."

Brock had allowed Pastor Gaines, Floyd, Tommie, Ditto *and* Deuce, to hear their conversation. It was important that they all knew why this young man behaved the way he did. After he finished the conversation, he spoke to their minds, *"Like Hope and Hans, some neglected children will act out to get attention. Any kind of attention."*

"Don't I know it," Gaines commiserated. *"As mannish as he is, thank God he ran to the church, instead of the gangs, like I did."*

Floyd and Brock nodded. Then Floyd said, *"I'll wager that boy has never had a girlfriend, let alone sex."*

"You are right, Floyd. Dr. Norris really should be ashamed of himself. He's so busy trying to save everybody else's family, but he has neglected his own."

Tommie immediately said, *"I will speak with Jaheem and find out his address."*

"We will go by his house and speak with his mother about allowing her sons to join our boys club," Ditto injected.

The entire conversation both angered and saddened Deuce. Even though his father was gone for months on in, his grandfather, uncles, and cousins had stepped up. Not to mention his big brother, Sam. *"I will have a heart-to-heart talk with Dr. Norris."*

"That's good. That's real good."

†††

Once Mark saw that Brock and that young man had stopped talking, he instructed, "Before they bring your dinner, please notice the gift cards on each of your chargers." Then he smiled and said, "Merry Christmas."

Jaheem reached for his card, but his reach was obstructed by Tommie's hand. "I'll take that, son."

Jaheem's continence fell. "I don't get one, like everybody else?"

"None of the children do. However, I will be glad to give it, and the one I received, to your parents. I am sure they will put it to better use."

"They're not here."

Ditto walked up. "We'll take you home, after dinner."

Jaheem went to respond, but he was drowned out by all of the screams and shouts. Then one shouted, "There's twenty-thousand dollars on my card!"

"Mine too!" another shouted.

"Is this amount for real, Pastor Gaines?" Benny asked. "Seriously?"

Gaines nodded and smiled. "It's a gift from Floyd's church, Redeeming Love. Merry Christmas, Brotha Benny."

Jaheem's eyes welled, as he stood up and hugged Tommie and Brock. Then he made his way to Floyd. "Thank you. I'm sorry I acted out."

Floyd's own eyes teared, as he hugged the

---

boy. "You were just trying to get someone to pay attention to you, son. I'm afraid you may have gotten more than you bargained for."

Everybody in the hall wiped their eyes and laughed.

Then he hugged Alden. "I'm sorry for what I said to you, in your office. I don't even have a girlfriend."

Alden hugged him and said, "I know you don't. Come by and talk with me, next week."

"You said Galilee wasn't open next week."

"I'll make an exception just for you. Anytime! *Every time!*" Then he pulled away from him and gave him his cell number. "Call me anytime."

Jaheem hugged him again. Little did this pastor know, he was going to *live* at Grace.

†††

"Dinner is served," H announced, as he and the men began to place the frosted crystal plates on the chargers.

Hope's crew followed behind them, with gravy boats. "Would you like some gravy on your dressing, son?" Daphne asked.

Jaheem looked at her and asked, "Does it have chicken gizzards in it?" He hated gizzards too. Actually, he hated gizzards, chitlins, pig feet, pig tails, and pig ears. He loved chicken, ham, pork chops, and bacon though.

"No, it doesn't. It has chopped up *chicken* in it."

"Yes, ma'am, I'd like some," he politely responded. Then he looked down at his plate and smiled. It was dressing, *two* slices of ham, *half* a chicken, candied yams, greens, macaroni and cheese, cranberry sauce, buttered rolls, *and* cornbread. With so many siblings, his plate had *never* been this full. He looked up at Brock and said, "No *chitlins!*"

Brock had been listening to his thoughts. He was sure with fourteen mouths to feed, it was hard keeping enough food on the table. He knew the gift card would come in handy. He went to castigate Dr. Norris in his mind, but he heard Michael speak to his mind, *"Dr. Norris works a lot of hours, but he has two jobs. One at the hospital, and the other teaching at the medical school. The second job pays for his siblings' college educations. He has already put four of them through college. He and those four are putting the next three through college right now, son."*

Brock was more than impressed with that family's strategy. *"That's well and good, but he needs to give his siblings attention."*

"He is only one man. Plus, he has found the love of his life, Cree. Maybe you should offer to ease his burden."

"I'll do just that," Brock replied. Then he turned his attention back to Jaheem and teased, "If you'd used your sense of smell you would've known there wouldn't be, because chitlins stink. You and everybody else would've smelled them in the

sanctuary."

Jaheem genuinely laughed. He had never been happier than he was in this moment. All he ever wanted was to be *noticed*. He tasted the dressing and moaned. Then he said, "My momma's don't taste nowhere near this *good*."

Everybody in the hall had the same thought, and each and every one of them asked for seconds. When they finished eating dinner and dessert, the women insisted on meeting Dee. She came to the hall, with her crew. Little did any of them know, she'd only cooked *one pan* of every dish. Chef had replicated them with his mind, over and over again. Everyone in the hall stood up and gave *them* a standing ovation. "Magnifico," Lula complimented.

"Outstanding," Ms. Margaret praised.

Even the men were impressed. "You are one lucky Dawg, nephew," Jorge shouted at Aden. "Cree is going to hate she missed this."

"In more ways than one, Uncle Jorge."

They all laughed. Even though dinner was over, no one was ready to leave. And that was a good thing…

†††

Although the adults were given gift cards, the children were not. Lizzie and Hans had taken it upon themselves to provide them with gifts.

"Hold on everybody," Justina shouted and clapped to get their attention. Then she announced, "My cousins and I have gifts for the children."

"Not for our cousins though," Ireland injected. Then she put her hand over her mouth when Justina glared at her. Everybody who knew how bossy Justina was laughed.

Brock arched his brows and mumbled, "What?" Then he looked at the tree behind the children's tables. Mounds of gifts were on the floor, out of view. He looked at his sneaky oldest twins and smiled. *"That's good, girls. That's real good."*

Although Jodi's dimples went in deep, her eyes welled. She whispered to their minds, *"I am so proud of you girls."*

"It was Ahyoka's and my idea," Sassy insisted.

"And mine too," Lil' H added.

"It was all of our idea," BJ insisted.

"They are all lying in church, Daddy," Hans tattled.

"They came up with the idea, but Hans and I came up with which gift to give each one. All of our cousins helped us wrap them," Lizzie explained.

"We're proud of all of you guys," Brock spoke to all of the children's minds.

All of the children from the estate stood up and started singing, "We wish *y'all* a Merry Christmas. We wish *y'all* a Merry Christmas." Sassy and Ahyoka danced around them, while Sheila, Sylvia, and the teens passed out the gifts.

The homeless children ripped the paper off their gifts and threw the wrapping paper on the floor. It appeared that all of them got what they wanted. They were hugging their gifts like they'd never received one and shouting, "Thank you!"

Autumn walked over to Jaheem and said, "Even though you're sitting with the adults, you're still our age." Then she smiled, handed him a gift, and said, "Merry Christmas."

Jaheem could not believe that with this many people in this hall they *noticed* him. Plus, she was too cute for words. He smiled, accepted the gift, and said, "Thanks." Then he opened it and saw it was the Nike shoes he wanted. He looked back up at her and added, "A lot!"

"You want to hang around, and help us teenagers take the trash bags out, and sweep the floor?"

His eyes were glowing, with a teenager's crush. "Yes!"

Brock noticed E staring at Autumn and Jaheem. He looked towards the kitchen to see Chef standing in the doorway, with his arms folded. Leroy was standing next to Chef, up against the wall, frowning. He leaned over, pointed at them, and warned, "You better behave yourself. That's her father, grandfather, and uncle watching. They heard what you said in church about tappin' your girlfriend. Trust me, they will *kill* you *dead.* Then ask God to forgive them, the moment you take your *last* breath." Then he burst out laughing at how big Jaheem's eyes got.

Everybody began to hug and slowly disburse when the teenagers started cleaning up. Alden shook Floyd's hand and praised, "What an amazing celebration. You know that they will be looking forward to celebrating in this same manner next year."

"I'm sure they will be," Floyd agreed. "We'll have to see what we can do."

†††

The men saw the teenagers struggling with the heavy trash bags. They and the field Watchers decided to lend them a hand. That's when Brock finally noticed that three of his Watchers were not there.

"X! Where are Zakzakiel, Lahabiel, and Jaoel? Didn't you tell them that I said they had to attend?"

"You know I did. They arrived on the bus with the soldiers. They just didn't come inside."

"Why not?"

"Come on, man. You know why."

Brock added them to the conversation. *"Z, L, J! It appears you guys found a loophole in my instructions. Get your butts to the rear of the church and help take out the trash! Now!"*

Zakzakiel, Lahabiel and Jaoel were stretched out on the bus. Z and L sat up and grunted. "That must mean it's finally over," J surmised.

"It's about time," Z griped.

"Let's get this over with so we can get out of

here," L stated.

They walked off the bus and made their way to the back door of the church.

CHAPTER 26

Z, L, and J saw a line of men tossing bags in the dumpster. Then they noticed two teenage boys dragging the bags on the ground. "Here, let me take those," Z offered and reached for the two bags.

Jon and Jas knew they were Watchers, and gladly handed them over. "With this many people, there are a lot more," Jon warned.

"We'll take them from the door to the dumpsters," L advised him.

"Thanks," Jas said. Then he and Jon ran back in the church to gather more.

Smooth, Angel, Greg and Ev walked out of the door carrying two bags each, as Jon and Jas ran back in. "We'll take those too," J said, as he and L grabbed them.

"Just pile them at the door. We'll be back to get them," L instructed. They slightly turned to go towards the dumpster but stopped mid-turn. Then they looked at each other and back at the door.

†††

Lynne, Vee, and Regina were over the cleanup crew. They refused to let the teenagers do all of the heavy lifting. They were grunting, while carrying the bags. The minute Lynne crossed the threshold, her eyes bugged, and she abruptly stopped. Vee almost ran in to her back. "Keep going, Lynne. This bag is heavy."

Lynne eased to the side, but she didn't divert her eyes away from Zakzakiel. Vee walked out the door and froze in her tracks. That caused Regina to bump into her. "What is it?" she asked.

Veagas wordlessly stepped to the right of the doorway but kept staring at Jaoel. Regina gazed ahead to see what her sisters were looking at. She gasped as her eyes locked with Lahabiel's. She mumbled, "At last."

They and the Watchers dropped the trash bags they were carrying, and slowly moved towards each other. The bags burst open and spilled on the ground, but none of them noticed. Ev knew what was happening, and he was not ready for this. His heart raced and he shouted outloud, "BROCK!"

†††

Brock was in the hall being introduced to Lula, along with his and Doc's team. He had not been in attendance at Grace, when Akibeel first fell in love with her. Nevertheless, he saw why he had. The two of them had the same *need to give back* spirit. The sound of her voice was even comforting to *his* ears. He'd wondered why Alden hadn't made her a deaconess but just hearing her talk revealed that wasn't her calling. Lula was a teacher, plain and simple. "My son speaks very highly of you, Lula. You have captured his heart."

"Kibee, Maria, and Mateo are my daily gentle breeze," she avowed. "It's so good to finally meet you, Brock. He always talks about how you rescued him from Hell. Thank you for doing that. *Our* son was worth rescuing. Wasn't he?"

He nodded, smiled, and went to verbally agree, but he heard Ev's shout. He chuckled and spoke to all of the Watchers that were still inside the hall, *"Look out back."*

They did and roaringly laughed in his mind. *"You ain't even right, Dawg!"* Donnell accused but kept laughing.

"If they'd brought their butts inside, it would've been a nice sideshow," X mused and kissed Cheryl's cheek.

"Ain't that the truth, but I'm glad that I didn't have a crowd!" T admitted. Cinquetta had been too traumatized for an audience to witness their meeting.

"Our way was better though. I didn't want a crowd looking on when Julia and I found each other," G injected.

"I'm just glad I didn't have Tamika's daddy frowning at me, like Everett is doing to those birds," O said and roared when she punched him.

†††

Brock had already forewarned Karen and Cora as to what was *about* to happen. Cora handed

Streeter off to Jodi, and they both were on the run towards the backdoor. Karen tripped and stumbled up a few of the stairs, but she kept going. That was a good thing because Cora ran right around and past her! They breathlessly ran out the backdoor, just in time to see them drop the trash bags. Cora ran to Greg and laughed. "Look at Daddy's face. He is *pissed!*"

Greg wrapped his arm around her and said, "You are right! I'm glad I didn't get that look." They both cracked up laughing.

Karen rushed over to Ev, wrapped her arms around him, and gleefully shouted, "FINALLY!"

Everett wrapped an arm around Karen, without taking his eyes off their daughters, as they walked into their 'Spirit' mates' arms. Karen was excited, but he was *not.* "They look like they are in their early twenties, but you and I both know they are not. Those dudes are over five thousand years old, and too damn old for our daughters, Karen."

"That don't matter, Everett. Their union was ordained by God, in the ages," she rebuked and elbowed him.

He grunted, and then he shouted again, "BROCK!"

Brock furrowed his brows and asserted, *"They are twenty-one-year-old young ladies, who have never been on a date. They've known all along that they were 'Spirit' mates. They are also aware that I knew who their mates were. They are lonely and have quietly blamed me for their loneliness. Not you! ME! All of them have a right to find happiness, instead of babysitting while we enjoy ours, Everett. And you know I'm right. My men are as lonely as your daughters are. Lonelier. They also know that I've known all along who their mates were. They are angry with me because I connected X, G, T and O with their mates a few years ago. I held off on these birds to appease you, Everett. But tell me something. If now wasn't a good time, when would've been?"*

"You should've warned me and their mother."

"I warned you three years ago, when I asked you if you were ready. You said no, so I honored your wishes. However, you had to know that El Roi wasn't going to allow me to hold off forever. You should've been preparing yourself, man," Brock reprimanded. *"Besides, Karen seems fine with it. You are the only one who has a problem. I know that you would've never been ready for this moment. Trust me, I get it. I wasn't ready for Aurellia to get married. I damn near lost my friggin mind when Baby Girl got pregnant. Remember? And don't forget, I've got three more daughters too."*

"I'll remind you when your turn comes around again," Ev threatened. Then he and Karen walked over to their girls. He didn't waste no time laying down the law. "I don't care if you are 'Spirit' mates. You cannot marry my daughters today, tomorrow or the day after either! In fact, don't even *think* about marrying them until *I* tell you to think about it."

"Daddy!" the girls and Cora shouted.

"Well damn, Everett! Just chill out," Smooth voiced and roared. "Keep in mind they can elope, if you don't loosen up, man."

Ev ignored his daughters and Smooth and kept laying down his law. "You all are going to properly date my daughters. And if by chance you decide to do what my brother just suggested, I will shoot all three of you the moment you return. Y'all understand me?"

Darious walked out the door in time to hear Ev's threat. He howled and mocked, "They are not Demons, man. Shooting them won't kill them."

He turned around, glared at Darious, and said, "If you remember, like you, I never shoot to *kill!* But I promise they will know that they've been shot."

Darious roared and said, "They may not die, but they will cry!"

Everybody in the backyard roared, even the three Watchers. Smooth laughed but then warned, "Since shooting you won't kill you, he'll probably do it every time he sees you."

"Y'all better listen to my brothers," Ev advised.

Brock had opened a link so everyone who lived on the estate could not only hear but see. The laughter was so loud, it was deafening. Jeremiel was also watching and listening. He was also allowing his father-in-law to witness it. He howled and said, *"Man, that dude sounds like you and Eric, Melvin."*

Melvin Foster *and* Eric George roared. *"I've always liked that cat. I can't wait to see how this romance evolves,"* Eric responded.

Z, J, and L smiled. They were okay with Ev's demands, because they wanted to get to know their mates. And their families. L squeezed Regina's hand and said, "We would never attempt to marry our mates without yours and their mother's blessing."

J was all for waiting because they had no home to take their mates to. He frowned. *"Who's going to stay with the soldiers, X?"*

"I'll get O, G, and T to drive them home. We'll work the other out later. Just concentrate on your woman, Dawg."

Z squeezed Lynne's hand and declared, "We have waited forever for our mates. None of us have a problem romancing them, and *celebrating with grace*, Everett."

†††

Jared and Floyd had heard what was going on. They walked out the backdoor in time to hear the end of the conversation. Floyd looked at the three Watchers and said, "First of all, you gentlemen no longer have an excuse as to why you don't come to church. Starting Sunday, I expect to see all three of you in the congregation, on the estate, sitting next to your mates."

They'd been mad at Brock for so long, they hadn't wanted to come anywhere near him, or his estate. They smiled because now they couldn't *wait*.

They nodded and agreed. "We'll be there," Z promised. Then he sent a shout out to Brock, *"Thanks, man."*

"You're welcome. I'm sorry it took me so long to do this. I was trying to give their father time to accept it," Brock explained.

"That cat's not happy, is he?"

Brock roared and kissed Lula's cheek. Then he said, "I need to get out back and see about my men. I will see you next week at Kibee's spot."

Lula was in love with Brock and all of these warriors of God. She hugged him and said, "I cannot wait."

Mateo, BJ, Kenny, and Lil' H ran over to her. Then Mateo said, "These are my cousins, BJ and Kenny. Today is our birthday."

"Well happy birthday boys."

"And this is our uncle Lil' H. Can they come with me the next time I come to your house?"

"Sure, baby," she agreed and hugged all of them.

All of the Watchers kissed her cheek and made the same promise that Brock made, including Akibeel.

†††

Brock was still laughing when he and his team walked out the door. Then he said out loud, "Everett will get over it!"

Jared saw the mess in the yard and visibly cringed. "Second of all, y'all can start proving yourselves by picking up all of this trash."

Vee couldn't help but chuckle. "That's our pastor, Jared. He's a neat freak."

"Then we'd better make haste. I don't want to upset God's man," Z replied.

"Otherwise he might refuse to marry us," L added.

"That's whenever Everett tells us we can think about it," J mocked and roared.

Everybody in the backyard laughed and started to help them. Jared laughed too, but he made no attempt to help. He shamelessly explained, "Sorry, I don't do other people's trash. But be sure to clean it all up."

That made them all laugh that much harder.

Alden, Capri, their spouses, and families walked out the back door to get in their cars. They paused long enough to say their good-byes. "We would stay and help but we've been invited to Erica and Ariel's to celebrate with the Archangels," Alden informed them. This was his first time meeting the other Archangels, and he was ecstatic. Everybody could hear the excitement in his voice.

"I still have a key. We'll lock up when they finish cleaning up the hall and kitchen," Floyd assured him.

Alden smiled. "Will talk with you soon."

Just as that crowd left, Tommie and Ditto walked out with Jaheem. "We'd help but we're taking him home," Tommie explained.

"Will you make sure that my father and mother take Na-omi and Lil' Henry home, Uncle Brock?" Ditto asked.

"We got them," Brock assured him. Then he extended his hand to Jaheem. "I am sure I will be seeing you soon, son."

Jaheem didn't accept his hand. Instead, he hugged him. No one had ever paid this much attention to him and he didn't want it to end. All of the teenagers told him that Brock was like that with all of them. And that he didn't treat them like their opinions didn't matter. "Thank you for *seeing* me, and *talking* with me, *Uncle* Brock."

Brock smiled because it never failed. He pulled away, teasingly squinted, and asked, "Who told you to call me *Uncle* Brock?"

Jaheem blushed and tattled, "Autumn. She said *everybody* calls you Uncle Brock."

Brock patted his back and roared. "Go on home now. But remember what I said about her father, uncle, and grandfather."

Jaheem laughed and tattled again, "*They* warned me. They also said that I can call her on the phone, or come visit her, if I behave myself."

Brock roared. "I bet they did. You'd better listen, boy," he said and kept laughing.

✝✝✝

When they drove around the corner, Brock looked inside the church and saw that all the congregation was gone. He look further and spotted several field Watchers driving the buses with the soldiers and homeless on them. He sent them a shout out, *"Come to the estate after you drop them off."*

Then he spoke to all of his peeps' minds, *"We need to get home so that we can celebrate our Christmas babies birthday. I'll clean up the church and lock the doors."* Then he teleported everybody to the spa and playroom, and their vehicles to the estate.

MESSAGE FROM AUTHOR

Sorry about leaving you guys with this cliffhanger. I couldn't help myself. No worries though. These three "Spirit" mates, along with a couple more, will have an old fashion romance and love story in an upcoming book. Until then, take time to read upon the real life of the once enslaved eleven-year-old *Benjamin Butts*.

Remember while you are celebrating Jesus's birth, to celebrate why our Savior came. Merry Christmas from me and my family to you and yours.

Turn the page to see all of the books in my catalogue, in the order they should be read. As well as books by some of my favorite authors.

BOOKS BY AUTHOR

TWO *SPIRITUAL* PARANORMAL SERIES
A *SPIRIT MATE* LOVE STORY
&
A *SANCTIONED MATE* SERIES

Brock's Redemption - #1
Ramiel's Symphony - #2
Denel's Lilia - #3
Chaziel's Hope - #4
Batman's Robyn - #5
Bezaliel's Destiny - #6
Arakiel's Faith - #7
Weddings & Births - #8
Baraquel's Dawn - #9
Henry's Pia - #10
The Brothas and the Greatest Gift - #11
Separate Vacations - #12
Yomiel – This is my story - #13
Adam – Beginnings & Revelations - #14
The Promise – Forbidden Loves - #15
The Wrath of Seraphiel - #16
The Walker Brothers – Then and Now - #17
The Archangel Michael - #1
The Archangel Araciel - #2
The Kingpin's Vitriol - #18
Much Ado - #19
The Archangel Chamuel - #3
Rogue's Rage - #20
TEKEL – The Weight of Mercy - #21
The Archangel Jeremiel - #4

EJ Brock
CELEBRATING WITH GRACE

The Archangel Ariel - #5
Brock's First Noel - #22
Forsake All Else When Love Is Ordained - #23
Lucifer's Lament - #24
Samson's Issues – The NAZARITES - #25
A Season For Giving - #26
Beyond The Shadow of Death - #6
Half My Spirit – All My Love - #27
The Archangels Jophiel and Raguel - #7
A Holiday in the Motherland - #28
Battered Road to Restoration - #29
Redeeming Love - #30
Darious, He Aims to Maim - #31
Before The Beginning - #0
Christmas at Grace Tabernacle - #32

CONTEMPORARY ROMANCE SERIES

An Outlandish Bid - #1
Loving Taylor - #2

STAND ALONE

In the Corridors of My Mind

COMING SOON

A Love With Waiting For
The Archangel Zadkiel
The Archangel Sammael

W Parks Brigham
Love Slipped In
Chance Encounter With Love
You're The One For Me
This Feels So Good

Michelle Evans
"It's Real in These Spiritual Streets"
Wife and Mistress #1
Duplicity Denied - #2
Memoirs of a Mistress - #5
Risky Pursuit - #4

Angelia Vernon Menchan
Christmas with Jake Sears
She was Born With A Veil
Always More Than Temptation

Iris Bolling
The Society Intellectual Beings
Jade
A Heart Divided

K. K. Harris
Black's Heart

Made in the USA
Middletown, DE
30 January 2022